The Celestial City

STANDING IN HOLY PLACES

BOOK TWO

THE CELESTIAL CITY

BY CHAD DAYBELL

Provo, Utah

This is a work of fiction and is not an official publication of The Church of Jesus Christ of Latter-day Saints. The characters, names, incidents, and dialogue are products of the author's imagination and are not to be construed as real.

ISBN 13: 978-1-932898-27-9
e. 1

Published by:
Spring Creek Book Company
P.O. Box 50355
Provo, Utah 84605-0355

www.springcreekbooks.com

Printed in the United States of America
10 9 8 7 6 5 4 3 2 1
Printed on acid-free paper

Library of Congress Cataloging-in-Publication Data

Daybell, Chad, 1968-
The celestial city / by Chad Daybell.
p. cm. -- (Standing in holy places ; bk. 2)
ISBN 978-1-932898-27-9 (pbk. : alk. paper)
1. Mormons--Fiction. 2. Second Advent--Fiction. 3. Imaginary wars and battles--Fiction. I. Title.
PS3554.A972C45 2008
813'.54--dc22

2008024383

Author's Note

As I did in the first volume, I want to emphasize that this series is a work of fiction. While the events portrayed in the book are based on scriptural prophecies and the words of the prophets, the specific locations mentioned in the book were selected based on my knowledge and familiarity with these areas, rather than a prophecy or account that targets these particular cities.

The only exception is the city of Independence in Jackson County, Missouri, which is identified in D&C 57:1-3 as the location where the Saints will build New Jerusalem in the near future.

This project will be a five-volume series, and each volume is outlined to include key events leading to the Second Coming, as well as provide a general overview of how these events will affect typical LDS families.

It is my hope that when readers finish the series, they will have a solid understanding of what lies ahead for the Saints. Then as these events actually occur, readers will recognize them, follow the counsel of the living prophet, and be able to respond appropriately, according to their own circumstances. Of course, my goal is to complete the series before these events actually occur!

For the most part I have purposely avoided specific details about the great destructions that await the wicked. Entire volumes could be written on that aspect alone, but it is my sincere hope that the readers of this series will be "standing in holy places" at that time and not be directly affected by those tragedies.

Instead, I have chosen to focus on events that will directly involve the Saints. There will be trials for each member of the Church in the coming years, but there will also be wonderful triumphs and blessings.

I want to mention two books that were helpful in structuring the storyline of this volume. The book *His Return: Prophecy, Destiny, and Hope* by Richard N. Skousen is a wonderful compilation and commentary from an LDS perspective on the prophecies and events related to the Second Coming.

The second book is *The Hopi Survival Guide* by Thomas Mails. It is an excellent summary of the history, traditions, and beliefs of the Hopi people, and was written with the approval of the tribal leaders.

I give special thanks to the helpful editors who do such an excellent job in strengthening each of my novels. I am grateful for your efforts and for saving me from embarrassing mistakes.

Finally, thank you for the many positive comments about the first volume of this series, and I sincerely hope you enjoy this next volume as these families move another step closer to the Savior's Second Coming.

Chad Daybell
June 2008

Moving Forward

Nearly six months had passed since the president of the LDS Church had given his historic message to the Saints gathered at the base of the Manti Temple. After the prophet's departure to an undisclosed location in the Rocky Mountains, the Saints in Manti and the surrounding towns stayed busy harvesting and storing the last portion of the abundant crop the valley's fields had produced that autumn.

While several women watched over the youngest children, everyone over the age of five was organized into teams and put to work picking the fruits and vegetables. The produce was brought to the cultural halls of the valley's meetinghouses, where Saints formed assembly lines to bottle and can the food. Each family took a fair portion of the food back to their homes, while extra food supplies were kept at each of the meetinghouses.

Meanwhile, the men and older boys worked as teams in the nearby canyons to cut down trees and haul loads of firewood back to the valley. Soon there were giant piles of cut firewood stacked under pavilions near the meetinghouses. These piles were covered with large plastic tarps in preparation for winter.

Halloween slipped by without notice as everyone worked together to winterize their homes, patching any leaky roofs and sealing drafty windows. They completed these tasks just in time, as the weather took a dramatic turn for the worse in early November. The westerly wind pattern known as the jet stream suddenly shifted south for a prolonged period. The jet stream typically would alternately shift north and south, bringing a variety of weather to the nation. But now it settled into a constant pattern above the California-Mexico border, crossing Arizona, Texas and the Gulf Coast, then moving across Florida as far south as Miami.

Such a shift in the jet stream had happened in Europe in the summer of 2007, leading to serious flooding and major damage there. This newest shift, however, was more severe and devastating, bringing frigid air from the arctic regions into most of the United States. After two weeks, snow blanketed nearly every city, and the northern half of the country was buried by a steady stream of blizzards and ice storms.

The jet stream would occasionally shift north for a couple of days, but usually only long enough to clear the skies and bring mild temperatures. Then it would shift south again, turning the melting snow into another layer of ice when the next storm arrived.

The city of St. George, Utah had received a startling six feet of snow by Thanksgiving Day, and across the nation water pipes froze, power lines snapped due to the ice, and snowdrifts on the sidewalks and roadways made even walking across the street a difficult task. The winter weather came as a mixed blessing for the United States, since it served as a form of protection from the Coalition forces that had invaded the nation the previous fall.

Those soldiers had made steady, methodical progress inland from both the Atlantic and Pacific coasts during October, and with the U.S. government crumbling without much of a fight, the Coalition leaders felt assured of victory. Their ultimate plan remained to exterminate the Americans, but to keep the cities intact so that their own people could soon come across the ocean and repopulate the land.

In accordance, after the initial attacks on the coastal cities, the Coalition soldiers had served more as cattle drivers, rather than act in open aggression that would destroy buildings and property. They moved at a steady pace through the streets, allowing the hoards of Americans in urban areas along both coasts to flee ahead of them and look for safety inland. The soldiers only fired their weapons when an occasional group would stand up against them, and those battles were always in favor of the Coalition forces. Only a handful of Coalition soldiers had been killed by Americans.

The Coalition soldiers almost felt pity for the Americans, who were woefully unprepared to leave their homes, and millions of citizens were now wandering the icy streets looking for shelter with little more than the clothes on their backs. The constant cold weather and the large numbers of people scrambling from city to city created a health nightmare as a highly contagious flu-like illness spread quickly, killing thousands of people each day.

As the death totals climbed, bodies were left unburied, and there wasn't much time to mourn the loss of a loved one. Sadly, many people had mixed emotions over the death of a friend or family member, because it meant one less mouth to feed. Starvation was quickly becoming everyone's main worry. The giant hail storm of the previous August had destroyed most of the nation's crops, and there simply wasn't enough food for everyone.

No one had heard from U.S. government leaders since the invasion, and the citizens were simply left to fend for themselves, leading to a mob mentality that resulted in thousands of additional deaths through senseless violence. Commercial areas near freeway viaducts with fast-food restaurants and "big box" stores became crowded with people who were looking for food and shelter. But there hadn't been any food available there for days, and these areas became war zones as groups of thugs attacked helpless citizens.

The prophecies of LDS leaders such as Joseph Smith and John Taylor began to be fulfilled as families splintered. Brothers fought against brothers, and fathers battled their sons in the scramble for food.

Another crippling blow for the Americans came when the Coalition forces located the building in Washington, D.C. that contained the computer database of U.S. citizens that had received the government-sponsored microchip. Within hours the Coalition's technicians had the computers operating, and the GPS devices in each microchip clearly pinpointed the locations where the remaining citizens had gathered.

The Americans who had eagerly jumped at the chance to "get the chip" in order to cash in on government rebates were now like fish trapped in a barrel as the Coalition forces began marching directly to where they were hiding. The soldiers would simply march down the freeway, take the next exit, and work their way through a city, wiping out thousands of citizens in an afternoon. The citizens would put up a meager fight, but the battles were so one-sided that the Coalition essentially left entire communities without inhabitants.

The conquering of America had been progressing so well that the Coalition leaders made plans to round up any surviving Americans by late December and hold mass executions on New Year's Day as a symbol of their complete victory. Their troops completely controlled the United States east of the Mississippi River, and the chip monitors indicated that few people were still living along the Pacific coast.

The only obstacle stopping the Coalition's efforts were the continuous snowstorms. The Rocky Mountain states of Utah, Colorado, Idaho, Montana, and Wyoming were encased in ice and snow. The Coalition forces made several failed attempts to move along the freeways into those states, but they finally decided it wasn't worth the effort to battle through 20-foot-high snowdrifts and climb steep mountain passes.

Besides, the Mountain West was now apparently just a frozen wasteland. The chip-tracking computers detected the biorhythms of only a few hundred individuals still alive in the entire region, mainly clustered near Denver and Salt Lake. The Coalition leaders laughingly told each other that those unfortunate souls were probably living in caves like hermits and would be lucky to survive the brutal winter.

So as the new year began, the Coalition leaders told their forces to sit tight and wait until the weather warmed up to finish off any remaining holdouts, if there were any. Then they would all celebrate the downfall of America.

⁂

Of course, the Coalition leaders were completely unaware that in the Rocky Mountains there were thousands of Latter-day Saints who were alive and well. These Saints had refused to receive the microchip when the U.S. government had offered it to them, and now they were virtually invisible to the Coalition forces.

The Saints were gathered in more than a dozen major gathering places throughout the mountains, each situated on the grounds of an LDS temple or at specially prepared areas that had served as LDS girls camps before the invasion. There were also a few gathering places for the Saints at temples in other parts of the United States, such as Orlando, Atlanta, and Dallas. The Saints at those temples had been undisturbed by the invading army because everyone there was "chip-free."

The Saints were privileged on each Fast Sunday to hear a message from the prophet through the Church's satellite network. It provided a great spiritual boost to all of the Saints to hear assuring words that the Church was doing well and that the Saints had remained undetected. His first message had been given that December, and he joked that the Tabernacle Choir was going to move right ahead with the annual First Presidency Christmas Devotional. Then the camera went to a wider angle, showing he was alone with his counselors in the room. The Saints couldn't help but smile as he commented the Choir must have had a scheduling conflict.

The prophet's calm demeanor served to strengthen the Saints across the land, but during that same broadcast he did get quite emotional as he reported that to the best of their knowledge, all of the Saints who had originally accepted the invitation to gather to the tent cities the previous spring were accounted for. He said some faithful Saints had passed away since that time from natural causes, but that every LDS camp had remained undetected by Coalition forces. He credited the Saints' faithfulness and continual prayers as the reason for this protection.

The prophet would close each monthly message with the simple admonition to keep the faith. The prophet assured the Saints that the Church still had every intention of building the celestial city of New Jerusalem. He promised them that soon the Lord's hand would be evident to the people of the world and that the scriptural prophecies would all be fulfilled.

Living in this unique period of time are three LDS couples, all in their late 30s. The previous year was the most challenging of their lives, but also the most rewarding one. Here are their situations as this volume begins:

Tad and Emma North

The Norths now live near the Manti Temple after gathering there the previous autumn with a group of Saints from Springville, Utah. Their group was just one of nearly thirty groups that had traveled from smaller, temporary mountain camps to gather to Manti.

Once all of these groups had arrived in Manti, it was clear the Saints were facing a severe housing shortage. So Church leaders assigned families to specific homes throughout Manti and in nearby communities such as Ephraim, Moroni, and Spring City. Each home in the valley now held between two and four families.

It initially felt very crowded for everyone, and there was even some bickering among families who claimed they would rather just keep living in a tent. But as the cold weather began to set in, people adjusted to the crowded situation and got used to it. The Norths share a small, two-bedroom home in Manti with their relatives, the Daltons.

There hadn't been electricity in the valley's homes since November, when the heavy snow made it impossible to keep the lines operational. However, there are electrical generators at the temple that are used for meetings and other special occasions.

Tad is a former accountant who endured a crisis of faith during the past year that nearly cost him his family—and his life. But as this volume begins he has returned to full activity in the Church. He has been helping each day with his Elders Quorum's assignment to keep firewood stocked at each of the homes on their block.

Emma's assignment includes supervising the lunch preparation for the families in their household. She assists with the other meals and handles several other tasks, including helping with younger children. With the freezing temperatures and crowded conditions, there is a need for someone to help keep the Saints healthy and happy, and Emma excels at that.

The Norths' three children are handling their new situation quite well. David is now almost 18, Charles is 12, and Leah is 9.

Doug and Becky Dalton

Doug is Emma North's younger brother, and they have always had a strong bond. Becky and Emma are close friends, and as mentioned earlier, they are sharing a house with the Norths.

Doug served as his stake's Preparedness Coordinator prior to the nation's upheaval, and he was involved in the Church's planning and preparation for the tent cities and gathering places. This allowed him to work closely with President Johnson, his stake president from Springville.

Once the Saints were settled in Manti, President Johnson was asked to continue as a stake president over a portion of the Saints, and he called Doug to serve as his first counselor. As part of his new calling, Doug was ordained a high priest.

As part of the stake presidency, Doug frequently attends meetings in the temple, where the leaders receive instructions directly from the Quorum of the Twelve through the Church's network. Doug and his fellow leaders often leave the temple feeling exhilarated as they are informed of plans being laid to fulfill the Lord's prophecies concerning the Saints and New Jerusalem.

Meanwhile, Becky has been busy serving as a school teacher, a profession she held before the gathering of the Saints. Each weekday the nearby meetinghouse is turned into an elementary school, organized and staffed by several young mothers, as well as many grandmothers. The school's classes include all the basics—reading, writing, and arithmetic—but it is based on the Primary program.

Becky's son Justin attends a CTR 4 class that she teaches, and her daughter Heather, now two years old, is in a nursery class. Becky is nearing the end of her pregnancy, and although she suffered a painful illness when a toxic cloud settled on the group in Spanish Fork Canyon, she has recovered well with only occasional health setbacks.

The biggest event for the Daltons and Norths during the winter was the calling of Emma and Doug's parents, Mark and Michelle Dalton, to serve as guardian missionaries at the Provo Temple. As Mark and Michelle had gotten older, their health was suffering, and they were concerned about being a burden on their family when it came time to make the expected trek to Missouri.

President Johnson was aware of their feelings, and when he was notified about the need for an older couple to help watch over the Provo Temple, he immediately thought of the Daltons and contacted Church headquarters. The calling was approved, and Doug and Tad took the Daltons to Provo in a horse-drawn sleigh in early March.

They are one of five couples who are contentedly taking care of the temple and monitoring the grounds, which are surrounded by the Church's standard 12-foot-high electric fence that is powered by generators. The couples have a large food supply stashed in the temple basement, and as Mark told Doug, "As long as I have my rifle and a pile of bullets to scare off intruders, we'll be fine."

Josh and Kim Brown

Over the past year, the Browns have had the greatest lifestyle change among the three couples. After working as an attorney for several years, Josh was called the previous spring to serve as the mission president in Quetzaltenango, Guatemala. While there, he and Kim gathered together thousands of faithful Saints to the temple grounds following Hurricane Barton, a massive storm that devastated the area.

Prior to the hurricane, the Browns had met with Elder Smith of the Quorum of the Twelve, who called Josh to be a member of the First Quorum of the Seventy. The apostle also informed Josh that he would soon lead the remaining Saints in Quetzaltenango to the United States to assist in building New Jerusalem, fulfilling Book of Mormon prophecies. With the help of a servant of the Lord named Mathoni, Josh and Kim began their journey northward with the Guatemalan Saints the previous fall.

The group had originally planned to travel through Texas, but thankfully Josh was still able to receive daily reports from Church headquarters through his solar-powered laptop that was linked to the Church satellite network. He learned that as the economy of Mexico had fallen apart, millions of Mexicans had moved northward, leading to clashes along the U.S.-Mexico border that had spread throughout the southwestern United States.

At the same time, thousands of Americans had fled south to escape both the Coalition troops and the horrible winter weather. As all of these groups converged on the same area, it developed into a terrible, lawless situation that had led to millions of deaths.

In response, Josh and Mathoni had guided the Guatemalan Saints through less-inhabited regions of Mexico. They traveled cautiously toward the west as the turmoil really set in throughout North America. The group had been seen by many people during their journey, but they were such an imposing group that no one had dared approach them.

The Guatemalan group crossed into Arizona in early February through an empty border crossing at Nogales, then followed the freeway system through Tucson and Phoenix, finding those once-vibrant cities abandoned. The unusual position of the jet stream that had frozen most of the United States had also left the Arizona desert without rain, and the citizens had fled north in desperation after their taps went dry. It was surreal for Josh and Kim to be back in the United States and see neglected cities, vacant homes, and unusual sights such as baseball fields and golf courses with dead grass.

The group reached the city of Flagstaff and stayed there for two days to recuperate from their seemingly endless journey. Josh had hoped that the streams from the nearby mountains would be flowing, but they are dry.

Thankfully, Mathoni has been a huge help in finding obscure sources of water along the way, such as abandoned wells that he would tinker with and miraculously get functioning. But with 15,000 thirsty souls, they need a larger source of water.

Josh knows that if the group keeps heading north they will eventually reach Lake Powell, which he figures must be receiving steady runoff from the Colorado River. But the lake is still many miles away, and he's worried other less-civilized groups will also be living there.

Josh has been in steady communication with Elder Smith of the Quorum of the Twelve through the Church network, but the apostle's only counsel at the moment is to continue moving northward and follow the promptings of the Holy Ghost. Josh was hoping for more specific directions, but as April approaches all he can do is lead the group north out of Flagstaff onto Highway 89 and try to reach Lake Powell safely within a few days.

Now on with the story.

Chapter 1

As the sun crept over the mountain ridge on a clear March morning in Manti, Tad North was already walking to the pavilion near the church meetinghouse where the firewood was stored. He stopped on the ice-packed road to watch the sunlight strike the tower of the Manti Temple, and he found the scene uplifting.

Yes, the temperature was several degrees below freezing and he could see his breath swirling around him, but he was definitely happy. A quote popped into his mind from Lou Gehrig, a former baseball star for the New York Yankees, who had once said, "Today I consider myself the luckiest man on the face of the earth."

Tad smiled. "Sorry, Lou, but I own that title now."

In many ways, Tad was right. He knew he should be a dead man. The previous year he'd been working at a Salt Lake accounting firm when he had turned against the counsel of the prophet and had chosen to receive the government's microchip.

He didn't tell his wife Emma about the chip, assuring himself he had done it to keep his family financially secure, but within weeks his life had spun out of control. Emma found out about the chip, and combined with Tad's worldly attitude, she couldn't endure living with him anymore. She and the kids had moved out to live with her parents, frustrated and disappointed by his choices. Then when Tad tried to get his life back on track, he had to elude a vicious government agent who sought to kill him. In desperation, Tad had finally cut the chip out of his hand with a broken bottle.

At that memory, Tad looked down at his hand. The injury had healed, but he would always have a jagged scar that reminded him of the Lord's mercy in allowing him to be reunited with his family. So now he was back among the Saints with the assignment to haul firewood to each home on the block. It certainly wasn't a prestigious calling, but he relished every minute of it. He knew that even his own family didn't quite comprehend the terror he'd been through while they had been safely tucked away at the mountain camp in Hobble Creek Canyon, but that didn't matter now. The foot he had injured the previous year on West Mountain had finally healed properly, and now he only wanted to move forward with life.

Within ten minutes Tad finished stacking a load of wood onto a large sleigh and began pulling it back toward their house. His sons David and Charles usually helped him load the wood at the pavilion, but he had decided to let them sleep in this morning. Since the house they were living in was crammed full of adults and little children, the two boys had been asked to sleep outside in one of the large tents the group had brought with them.

He admired his sons' willingness to sleep outside, but sometimes after yet another crying child had awakened the entire household during the night, he envied them a little. After all, the boys wore very effective foam clothing that some Saints had created in the years before the Coalition invasion, and the clothing kept them amazingly warm, even when the temperature dropped below zero. Combined with their sleeping bags, Tad sensed that the boys were sleeping better than he was.

Once Tad reached the house, he went to the boys' tent, zipped open the tent flap, stuck his head inside, and called out, "Rise and shine! There's wood to be delivered!"

David sat up and rubbed his hands together to fight off the cold. "Whoa, the sun is already up," he said. "We're running late today."

Tad smiled. "I've already been to the pavilion and loaded the sleigh. I figured you needed to catch up on your beauty sleep. Isn't there a youth dance tonight? I'll bet there will be a few girls watching for you."

David laughed and said, "That's wishful thinking."

He climbed out of his sleeping bag and pulled his boots on. "Dad, since you've already gathered the wood, I'll take care of the deliveries. You go in and have a nice breakfast with Mom."

"Really?" Tad responded. "Thanks, son. I would appreciate that."

They glanced over at Charles, who was still huddled inside his sleeping bag. "Let him sleep," David said. "I'll be fine doing the route on my own."

As David pulled the sleigh around the block, he marveled at what a strange year it had been. Just twelve months before, he had been a junior in high school with plans to attend BYU and then serve as a full-time missionary. But then the world had changed dramatically. The prophet had called all of the missionaries home, and the Saints had gathered in the mountain camps. Then the destructions had begun—the earthquakes, the Great Storm, the flooding, and the invasion from the Coalition forces that had crushed the nation.

The current situation in Manti certainly had its challenges, but David felt like he was a better person than he'd been a year earlier. Previously, he had spent a lot of his free time playing video games or basically just goofing off with his friends at the South Towne Mall near his family's apartment in Sandy.

Now, as far as he knew, there wasn't a functioning video game in the whole city of Manti, and he realized now how many pointless hours he had devoted to that hobby. This new lifestyle where everybody had been asked to pitch in was keeping him busy all day, which made him surprisingly happy.

He did miss the social interaction of high school, but he had to admit that the fashions among the girls his age had become so immodest, even among his ward members, that he had worried about finding a righteous wife someday. But since living in the mountain camp and then traveling to Manti, he had met several wonderful girls who loved the gospel. Of course, immodesty wasn't currently an issue, since most of the time the girls were bundled from head to toe to keep warm.

David didn't know exactly what his future would hold, but he sensed that the Saints were on the brink of something very important. Many of the Saints in Manti felt they would be called to help build New Jerusalem, and he hoped that was true. Meanwhile, he would just keep doing his best to help out each day, even if that simply meant hauling a lot of firewood.

Tad watched David round the corner with the sleigh, then he went inside the house and found his wife Emma at the kitchen table, where she was peeling some potatoes for the household's lunch. Within moments they were joined in the kitchen by Doug's wife Becky.

"Tad, I'm glad you're here," Becky said. "Doug told me the leaders had a great meeting in the temple last night. He's eager to tell us about it. He'll be here in a minute."

Tad motioned toward Becky's bulging stomach. She was now nearly nine months along in her pregnancy, and everyone expected the baby to arrive any day.

"How are you feeling?" Tad asked.

"Not too bad, but the baby just won't hold still," Becky said. "I'm looking forward to some contractions."

Doug then entered the room and stood next to his wife. "Good morning, Tad. Are you back from hauling the wood already?"

"Well, David volunteered to take care of the route today, so I didn't fight him too hard about it."

Doug smiled. "I'm glad, because I have lots of news to share with the three of you. As you know, the satellite connection has been down, but the brethren were able to reconnect to the system yesterday, so we were able to find out what's been happening throughout the nation the past couple of weeks."

Doug's calling as a counselor in the stake presidency allowed him to attend top-level meetings with other priesthood leaders in the Manti Temple, and although he couldn't tell his family everything that was discussed there, he was able to share with them many details of what was happening in the world. The Church had many daring, adventurous members scattered across the land who were putting their lives on the line to sneak into the surrounding cities and then report back to the Church through the satellite system. Their reports helped the Church stay on top of situations around the nation.

"I'm glad they finally got the system fixed," Tad said. "What's been going on?"

"Well, the biggest surprise has been that the flu-like illness is still affecting both the Americans and the Coalition forces. We thought it had faded away in January, but now thousands of people are dying from a new outbreak. In fact, the Coalition forces are now gathering in just a few major cities in hopes of quarantining themselves and stopping the illness from spreading among them."

"It has been such a blessing that we've been fairly healthy here," Emma said. "It sounds like maybe the sickness is the Lord's way of slowing the progress of the Coalition army."

Doug nodded. "That's interesting you would say that, because during the broadcast one of the apostles gave his opinion that the illness was a fulfillment of D&C 45:31-32."

"What does it say?" Tad asked.

Becky grabbed a Triple Combination from a nearby shelf. "I'll read it," she said, flipping to the right page. "'*And there shall be men standing in that generation, that shall not pass until they shall see an overflowing scourge; for a desolating sickness shall cover the land. But my disciples shall stand in holy places, and shall not be moved; but among the wicked, men shall lift up their voices and curse God and die.*'"

They all paused in silence, realizing how accurately the scripture described their current situation.

"It is also interesting how other prophecies are coming to pass in rapid succession," Doug said. "The earthquakes here in the mountains have slowed down considerably and aren't nearly as powerful as they were last year. But apparently Manhattan was rocked by a monstrous earthquake. That area can't catch a break. First came the Coalition attack there last year, and now this latest devastation. The reports say the city is almost uninhabitable because most of the skyscrapers and apartment buildings came tumbling down and filled the streets with rubble. The tunnels under the Hudson and East rivers collapsed, and nearly all of the bridges are destroyed. Even the George Washington Bridge is now too unstable to cross. One of our scouts there reported that he had to swim across the Hudson to New Jersey to find food."

"That's terrible," Tad said. "It makes the collapse of the World Trade Center seem like nothing."

"That wasn't all that happened on the East Coast," Doug said. "A second earthquake a few miles offshore triggered a tsunami that flooded a great portion of the eastern seaboard, including Boston. Brigham Young had prophesied of these events more than 150 years ago, and now they have actually occurred."

Emma frowned slightly. The reports of destruction always made her feel a bit tense and nervous. "Is there any hope the invasion is going to end soon?" she asked.

"Well, since most of the Coalition army has moved toward the center of the country, they weren't affected by these earthquakes. But the good news is it doesn't look like the Coalition is going to send additional soldiers to America. We've received some reports that Russia and China aren't getting along now. They're blaming each other for the delay in conquering America and are actually having some battles along their own border."

"So things might be looking better?" Becky asked. "Maybe these problems won't go on forever."

"I don't know about that," Doug said. "It really looks like the United States government as we know it has collapsed. One of our spies living near the Washington D.C. Temple took a digital video camera and went down into the city for a couple of days. He sent back some footage, and all of the buildings are either abandoned or destroyed. He said there were many bodies decaying in the streets, but he didn't see another living person during the whole time he was down there. The White House has been burned, and even if the president is still alive somewhere, such as in a secret bunker in Virginia where some people think he went, he doesn't have a government to lead."

Emma shook her head. "It doesn't seem like we have many options left other than to just wait this out."

"That's exactly what the apostles told us," Doug said. "We just need to stay where we are and pray for protection and guidance."

Becky clutched her bulging stomach as the baby kicked again. "That sounds good to me. With this wild child inside of me, I can certainly use all the prayers I can get."

CHAPTER 2

At that moment a few hundred miles to the south, Becky's sister-in-law Kim Brown was helping a young Guatemalan mother feed her three children. Even though it was only mid-morning, Kim was exhausted and it took all of her strength to wrestle with the little boy she held on her lap.

She looked back down Highway 89 at a long train of scattered handcarts. They had left Flagstaff, Arizona the previous day, and thousands of Guatemalan Saints filled the road as they began to pack up their tents and prepare to start traveling north again. She greatly admired each of them, because this trip had been much more difficult than they could have imagined.

The journey through Arizona had been especially difficult with hot temperatures and water always in short supply. Kim's husband Josh had received reports from the Church that Utah and most of the U.S. was still suffering through frigid conditions, and she could hardly believe it.

As she watched these faithful Saints pack up their belongings, Kim remembered how the Church had always given honor and deep respect to the Mormon Pioneers that crossed the plains in the 1800s. However, she couldn't envision the travels of those early Saints being more severe than what this group was experiencing. The group had been on the move for more than five months, and the frustrating part was they really didn't have a destination yet.

When they had started their trek out of Guatemala the previous autumn, Kim fully expected them to move quickly through Mexico, cross into the United States without much opposition, and then triumphantly march to Missouri to begin building the New Jerusalem. How did Arizona fit into all of this?

Kim hoped Josh would return to the group that evening. He had gone ahead two days earlier with his friend Mathoni to evaluate the situation at Lake Powell. It terrified her that he had left her behind, but she knew that if they had encountered danger along the way, she would have been a liability.

"Heavenly Father, please watch over Josh," she prayed. "Surely there is a purpose for us taking this strange path to Zion."

Josh stood behind a boulder and peered through binoculars toward the town of Page, Arizona. The sight was frightening. He had expected to find people here, such as vagabonds looking for food and shelter, but not what he saw before him. Several thousand Coalition troops were camped throughout the town. They even had tanks and trucks blocking the roads.

Josh didn't know what to think. He turned to Mathoni, who was crouched next to him on the ridge. "How can we get around them to reach the lake?" Josh asked him. "We don't have many weapons, and if the troops spotted us, they would easily destroy our group. What do you recommend we do?"

"I'll do whatever you decide," Mathoni said.

Josh turned away in frustration. Mathoni had given him a similar answer several times during their journey when Josh was feeling a bit overwhelmed. Yes, Josh was a member of the First Quorum of the Seventy, but Mathoni was one of the Three Nephites! Couldn't he make a decision once in a while?

Then Josh reminded himself he was the one set apart to preside and make decisions for the group. Mathoni had explained to him that although he had been part of the Church leadership among the Nephite civilization, that Church organization had ceased to exist. So while Mathoni still held the priesthood, he didn't have a leadership role in the latter-day church.

The interesting thing for Josh is that no one else in their

group thought "Brother Mathoni" was anything more than a very dedicated worker. Some of the Saints had noticed he always completed his tasks quite quickly and had a real knack for finding water, but otherwise he hadn't given the others in the group any hint that he was actually a translated being.

"How many soldiers do you think there are?" Josh asked him.

"I would say there are about 8,000 of them."

"Well, our only option is to hurry back to the group and have them turn around," Josh said. "It will be frustrating for them, but it's better than getting everyone killed."

They started to move down the slope when they noticed a glint of sunlight reflected from a nearby hill. Josh grabbed his binoculars and focused on where the glint had come from. He soon spotted someone looking through binoculars back at him!

"We're being watched by someone," he told Mathoni as he ducked down. "But he doesn't look like a Coalition soldier. In fact, he's wearing a BYU hat!"

The men looked at each other in surprise. "Let me go talk to him," Mathoni said before quickly slipping away. Josh trained the binoculars again on the nearby hill, and within a few seconds he saw Mathoni standing behind the man.

"Sheesh, I wish I could move like that," Josh said under his breath.

Mathoni tapped the man on the shoulder, and the poor fellow was understandably shocked. Once he recovered from the surprise, he and Mathoni started talking, and from what Josh could tell, they were getting along like old buddies.

Within a few minutes Mathoni and his new friend began walking toward Josh. When they reached him, Mathoni introduced his friend by saying, "Elder Brown, this is Joseph Evehema, a leader among the Hopi people, a member of the Church—and a fan of the BYU Cougars. He has something to tell you."

Joseph and Josh shook hands, and then Joseph said, "Yesterday I climbed upon our sacred mountain, and the Spirit told me, 'There is a large group of Saints nearby who need your help. Go to them.

They are my people, and your brothers.' Then I was shown in my mind the ridge where we are now standing. I hurried here this morning, because I knew the enemy soldiers were camped in Page. But when I arrived here, all I saw were the enemy soldiers. I thought I had been deceived, but then I saw you two here. Certainly there are more of you?"

"Yes, there are about 15,000 Saints a few miles down the road," Josh said. "We were trying to reach Lake Powell, but that obviously isn't going to happen with the Coalition soldiers already here. Now I'm not sure why we were led in this direction."

"I know why," Joseph said. "I feel you were meant to come to our home, which we call Hopiland. We can help you, and I know that is what the Lord wants."

"Are you sure?" Josh asked. "We're almost out of food . . ."

Joseph raised his hand. "This past growing season we grew an abundance of corn, and we still have plenty stored away. We'll be able to give your people a nice place to rest and be well-fed."

Josh smiled and slapped Joseph on the back. "I like the sound of that. Let's get back to our group and away from these soldiers," Josh said. "It's a miracle their spies didn't see us."

"We worried about that too, but thankfully the soldiers are feeling too comfortable to worry about needing spies," Joseph said. "They killed the citizens who were here when they first arrived, and since then they've have been taking it easy."

A few hours later, the three men reached the Guatemalan group as it moved up Highway 89, and Kim rushed into Josh's arms. "Is everything going to be all right?" she asked.

"Yes, Brother Evehema has been guided by the Lord to assist us. He's going to take us to a place of safety among his people, the Hopi tribe."

Kim was thrilled by the news. She had never had a good feeling about Lake Powell, but now it looked like everything was going to work out. By the end of the day, Brother Evehema had led them away from Highway 89 and several miles down a quiet two-lane road to a small valley with a spring. Far off in the distance across the desert a series of towering mesas could be seen.

"We'll be safe here tonight, and within a couple of days we will reach Hopiland," Brother Evehema said, pointing toward the mesas.

Josh put his hand on Brother Evehema's shoulder. "Thank you so much," he said. "But how will your people respond to having several thousand people suddenly show up?"

"They won't be surprised at all," he said. "We are living through the Third Shaking that our people have long awaited, and we know the Lord will count on us to help many people."

"The Third Shaking?" Josh asked. "I've never heard of that."

"You have, but by a different name," Brother Evehema said. "It's also called the Third World War. Once everyone is settled in Hopiland, I will have the tribal elders explain more to you about our prophecies and what we expect in the future."

That night Josh pulled out his laptop and inserted one of his few remaining batteries. Then he sent a message through the Church network to his friend Elder Smith of the Twelve Apostles. He reported the discovery of the Coalition soldiers stationed in the city of Page, and he explained how Brother Evehema had come to their rescue.

Josh asked Elder Smith if he had any further information about the location of other Coalition troops that they should avoid. He also asked what the Guatemalan Saints should do now. The next day Josh received a response from Elder Smith. It read:

Several of the apostles met this morning, and I explained the situation that you and the Guatemalan Saints are facing. After much discussion and prayer, we feel you are in the right place at this time. Stay with our Hopi brothers and sisters for the foreseeable future.

The Church has property and a chapel in Hopiland in the town of Polacca, and you can use that building and the surrounding property as your base camp. We are confident the Hopis will welcome you with open arms.

As for the Coalition forces, from the data we can obtain, the soldiers in Page apparently are the remnants of the forces that originally landed in California. The harsh weather forced them south and east, causing them to gather first in Phoenix and now near Lake Powell. Stay clear of them, because they might be on the move again soon. We've had reports that the Coalition forces are going to gather into one large group, then wait for the snow to melt before attempting to finish off the remaining Americans.

The interesting thing is where the Coalition forces are gathering. Maybe it is pure coincidence, but we feel Satan is behind it. They are gathering to the same place we hope to go soon—the cities surrounding Jackson County, Missouri. Things are getting quite interesting, aren't they?

Josh closed his laptop and shook his head. "Elder Smith, you have always been the master of understatement."

Chapter 3

Coalition soldier Mitko Petrov stood quietly in the middle of a street in Kansas City, Missouri. He was tall with dark hair and light skin, like his Bulgarian father. He slowly rotated his body as he pointed a portable tracking device toward the nearby buildings. The small device was capable of locating anyone within 1,000 yards who had received the U.S. government's implanted microchip. It didn't matter whether people were hiding on the top floor of a skyscraper or were tucked away in an underground shelter—Mitko would find them.

Mitko's device was primitive compared to the larger chip-tracking scanners that could cover nearly a mile, but this smaller version served its purpose well as Mitko and a few of his fellow soldiers made a final sweep through this neighborhood. The city had been a bustling metropolis less than a year earlier, but the Americans had fled in terror from the advancing army. Now the Coalition soldiers were just checking for any stragglers.

As Mitko pointed the device at a vacant field, its red light began to flash slowly. Surprised, he moved into the field and the light flashed more rapidly.

"Hey, I've got something over here," he called out in his native language. Mitko and three other soldiers were soon standing in the middle of the field, surrounded only by weeds and a few shrubs. They were a bit perplexed as the device continued to flash. Then Mitko noticed a small shrub that didn't look quite right. He pulled the branches aside and noticed a hidden metal lid. Another soldier ripped out the shrub, then grabbed the lid's handle and yanked it upward, revealing a rickety wooden ladder that led down into a passageway.

A soldier shined a flashlight into the chamber to make sure it was empty, then the group climbed cautiously down the ladder, pistols in hand, with Mitko following behind. The passageway opened into a damp, small room that looked like it might have once been a part of the city's sewer system. The soldiers could only see solid concrete walls with no place to hide.

"Petrov, is that scanner working right?" one of the soldiers asked.

"It's still flashing like crazy," Mitko responded. He then went to a small vent cover on the far wall and wrenched it loose. He found himself staring into the eyes of a terrified American man.

"How did you find us?" the man cried.

Mitko pointed at the back of the man's hand, indicating the chip, and the man shook his head in frustration. "This thing has been nothing but a curse to my family," he cried.

The soldiers dragged the man out of the vent, as well as a woman and two children who had also somehow wiggled in ahead of him. The Coalition soldiers knew their orders—"spare no one"—and they would complete their task. Mitko was already halfway up the ladder as the gunshots echoed in the chamber. He didn't look back as the family was killed. He despised this part of the job and gladly left it to his blood-thirsty comrades, who actually enjoyed the experience.

Mitko was well-respected among his fellow soldiers, partly because he was in his mid-20s. Most of the Coalition soldiers were still in their teenage years. However, he carried a secret that would certainly have caused his younger comrades to treat him with disgust—this was actually his third time in the United States and he loved the American people.

Mitko was born in Bulgaria, but his parents had brought him

to Utah when he was a young boy. His father was earning a masters degree at BYU, and Mitko had fond memories of those carefree years, such as playing with a variety of neighborhood kids in the irrigation ditch near their apartment. His parents were members of the LDS Church, and Mitko had made many friends in Utah. He even learned English quite well at the nearby elementary school. But after three years, his father's student visa expired, and the Petrovs were required to return to Bulgaria.

Mitko was an only child, and his parents had every intention of returning to Utah so he could enjoy the higher standard of living the United States offered, but the years passed by fairly peacefully in their homeland. His father's advanced degree from an American university had landed him a prized job, and both of his parents were leaders in the Church in Bulgaria, so their dream of returning to Utah soon faded as they became fully involved in their ward there.

Then when Mitko was 19 years old, he decided to serve a mission for the Church. To his parents' great joy, he was called to serve in the Nebraska Omaha Mission. Mitko served a wonderful mission that included many baptisms, and he grew to love America all over again.

In his final proselyting area, he became close friends with a member of the stake presidency, Josh Brown, and his wife Kim. The Browns had never been able to have children, and they seemed to subconsciously adopt Mitko for a few months. Sister Brown had insisted that he and his companion do their laundry at their home each P-Day, rather than going to the laundromat.

Josh made it a point to come home early from work that day to be able to talk with the missionaries and get an update on how the work was going in their stake. Meanwhile, Kim always prepared for them a delicious dinner with plenty of leftovers that they took back with them to their apartment.

Throughout his mission, Mitko's parents had carefully saved their money so they could travel from Bulgaria to pick him up at the end of his mission. They were thrilled to be in America again, and the Browns traveled with the Petrovs for two days in Missouri to show them Church historical sites such as Liberty Jail, the Valley of Adam-ondi-Ahman, and the city of Independence in Jackson County.

As part of their tour, Josh said something that had stuck with Mitko. Josh had explained to the Petrovs the significance of the area as the future site of New Jerusalem. He added that the prophets had said the land would first be swept clean of its inhabitants before Zion could be built there.

They had discussed for several minutes how a cleansing could ever happen in such a large metropolitan area, and they hadn't come up with a solid answer. But now Mitko understood how such a cleansing could happen—he was participating in it.

Mitko's daily life in Bulgaria had been particularly difficult after his mission. He found himself working in a hot, dirty factory doing mundane tasks, and he missed the freedom and happiness he had enjoyed in the United States both as a young boy and as a missionary.

As the Coalition began to take shape and recruitment for soldiers began throughout Eastern Europe and Asia, Mitko felt trapped. He could stay in the dreary factory, or he could go to war. His parents considered helping him flee somehow to the United States, but after a long night of prayer and fasting by the whole family, Mitko's father gave him a blessing. The words still resounded in his head: "Mitko, the Lord has placed you in this position. You must join the Coalition forces, and the Lord will make you an essential tool in his hands."

Mitko reluctantly joined the Coalition army the following day, and he hadn't seen his parents since then. He also hadn't had any contact with the Church, and he felt prompted to just blend in and keep his past a secret.

His unit had been one of the first Coalition groups to reach U.S. soil, landing in South Carolina, but during their first few weeks in

America they hadn't been in a real battle. They had slowly worked their way west through major cities such as Atlanta, Chattanooga and Nashville, methodically driving the citizens across the land, and finishing off any citizens who couldn't stay ahead of them.

Of course, before the Coalition forces even arrived, the Americans had already done a good job of killing each other off during several weeks of civil unrest after their economy collapsed. The citizens who survived the riots had fled westward, so there really weren't many people left in those southern U.S. cities by the time the Coalition soldiers passed through.

Because of those circumstances, the reality was that Mitko had never actually killed anyone. Sure, he had put his rifle to his shoulder just like the other soldiers when they came across some stragglers, but he never pulled the trigger, and his commanding officers never checked to see if he had fired his rifle. He hated bloodshed and had promised the Lord he would never take a human life unless his own life was threatened. He had mixed feelings about having to operate the chip detector, but he hoped somehow the Lord would understand that it was a job he couldn't avoid.

Mitko had particularly bad memories of what had happened in November. After being chased halfway across the continent, thousands of citizens had banded together in Kansas City, Missouri, to put up a battle against the Coalition. But following a day of staggering losses, the citizens fled into Kansas, hiding themselves among fields of dried cornstalks.

The first major snowstorm of the year arrived that night, and most of the citizens froze to death in the fields. Mitko had been among the soldiers who had gone into the fields two days later to see if there had been any survivors. There weren't, and the images of entire families frozen together as they huddled in the snow were burned into his mind.

Meanwhile, the Coalition forces hunkered down in Kansas City to wait out the storm. The plan was to move west again when the skies cleared, with Denver as their next target. But the storms kept coming, and the Coalition forces stayed put.

❧ ❧ ❧

A week after Mitko had found the American family in the sewer system, the Coalition soldiers had completed their search of the area. Several other families had been found and eliminated by other units, and the soldiers felt satisfied there weren't any Americans remaining in the area.

Now all the soldiers could do was wait for the weather to improve. The flu-like sickness was again making a large dent in the Coalition ranks. There had been originally nearly 12,000 Coalition soldiers in Kansas City, but they were now down to 7,000. Mitko silently prayed day and night that he would avoid catching the sickness, and so far he had been among the healthiest soldiers. Unfortunately, this meant he had to help load the bodies of the dead soldiers into wheelbarrows and dump them off the end of a dock into a hole they had cut in the ice of the Missouri River, since the ground was too frozen to dig graves.

Mitko had taken up residence in a large office building along with several other soldiers, and they found if they stayed in the center of the building and kept all of the doors shut, the temperature stayed above freezing. Of course, some of the soldiers were burning whatever they could find to keep warm, but Mitko chose to just wait out the cold. It was mentally excruciating, so he would slip away from the building for hours at a time and find books to read. He hadn't yet found the grand prize—a Book of Mormon—but he had found a Bible, and the Savior's words had been comforting to him.

One day while the sun was shining Mitko walked for several blocks away from the city center. He never saw another soul—just the decaying remains of a society that had forgotten God. He spotted an LDS meetinghouse and went inside. The building was stripped bare, but it didn't appear vandalized. It gave him hope that the Saints in Missouri had been forewarned and had taken everything with them, even down to the hymn books and the sacrament trays.

He went into the chapel and saw a portable blackboard near the front. Enough sunlight was streaming in that he could see a list written on the board:

1. Organize as family groups with a designated leader and give your list of names to your bishop.

2. Make sure everyone in your group, including each child, has a backpack that contains a 72-hour kit and bottled water.

3. Each person is allowed two sets of clothing that must be packed in a standard suitcase with your family's name written on it. No cell phones, electronic games or other gadgets will be allowed.

4. The buses will leave tomorrow at 5 a.m. sharp. Sleep in the cultural hall tonight if needed.

5. Pray with all of your heart that we will be protected on the way to the camp!

Mitko felt a surge of relief as he pictured the chapel full of Saints heeding the call to gather to a camp where they could survive the Coalition invasion. He now knew that the Saints who had lived in Jackson County were now safely hidden away somewhere, waiting for the right time to return to build New Jerusalem.

In fact, as the Coalition forces had made their way along the freeways of the eastern United States, Mitko could remember at least five distinct times that he had seen the spires of an LDS temple within a mile of the freeway. He had purposely avoided drawing attention to the temples, and he believed the Lord had shielded the eyes of his fellow soldiers from seeing them.

The soldiers had typically taken the time to investigate skyscrapers or unusual buildings along the way, but the temples were always overlooked. Mitko was certain that if the soldiers had gone to those temples they would have found hundreds of Saints gathered on the grounds.

Another thing that had comforted him during their march across the United States was that he had never seen anyone that he would have classified as an active Mormon. Most of the Americans that met their fate at the hands of the soldiers were as un-Mormon as you could get, with unruly hair, angry faces, and a general slovenly unshaven appearance—and the men were even worse.

Yet Mitko felt a slight sense of pity for them. He imagined that the Nephites in their final days had a similar appearance as their actions drove the light of Christ from their lives.

A large number of the people who were killed wore shirts or hats that said "Budweiser" across them, and at first the Coalition soldiers wondered if "Budweiser" was some sort of resistance force. Then some of the soldiers found empty beer cans with that name on the side of them. From that point on, the soldiers sought to find some Budweiser of their own at each commercial center, but apparently every can of beer throughout the land had already been consumed.

Mitko left the meetinghouse and began walking back to the office building. As the sun set, he noticed a faded billboard on a nearby building. A beautiful couple smiled down with the phrase "*It's hip to get the chip!*" emblazoned above them. Mitko shook his head in frustration.

"You Americans had it all," he shouted at the smiling models. "Now everything is gone."

He thought of what he had witnessed over the past several months—unfathomable scenes of Americans fleeing for their lives who didn't hesitate to kill each other in order to stay ahead of the Coalition forces. Mitko frowned at those memories and looked around him, knowing the prophecy concerning the cleansing of Jackson County had been fulfilled. The area had certainly been swept clean by the thousands of Coalition soldiers gathered there. They had killed and eaten every animal larger than a rat, and now they had even started eating the rats, too. Once the Coalition army moved on, there wouldn't be a living thing left in Jackson County, other than a few snakes, mice, and spiders.

"Maybe I'm here to testify of this," Mitko told himself. He tried to imagine New Jerusalem someday rising from these ruins. It would take a lot of work, but he could see it happening.

"Heavenly Father," he prayed, "if possible, let me take part in building thy kingdom."

Mitko paused to reflect on where Josh and Kim Brown might possibly be. He figured they had left Nebraska since the invasion, but they had been so faithful that he was sure the Lord was putting them to work somewhere. As Mitko returned to the office building to rejoin the other soldiers, he could never have guessed the significant events that would bring him together with the Browns once again.

Chapter 4

On the last day of March, Doug Dalton was summoned to a special leadership meeting in the Manti Temple. As he sat next to President Johnson, there was a hint of tension in the air. The lights in the hall dimmed, and on a screen at the front of the room was a video image of the prophet standing at a pulpit, with several of the apostles seated behind him.

"My dear brethren, thank you for gathering in your various temples on short notice," the prophet said. "As you know, the Lord works on His own timetable, and He has given us new directions and guidance today. So I decided we better not putter around about it."

The prophet gave a smile, and the men in the congregation laughed. Doug was continually amazed at how calm and relaxed the prophet seemed. The Lord had certainly put the right man at the head of the Church during such a stressful time.

The prophet continued, "In all seriousness, based on reports from our brave 'maintenance missionaries' living undetected in various parts of the country, the Coalition forces appear to have nearly completed moving all of their smaller groups into one large army near Kansas City. Their forces have been hit hard by the fierce winter and the severe illness that has taken the lives of so many of our countrymen, but they do currently control the rest of the United States outside of the Rocky Mountain region. It appears they are just waiting for the snow to melt, and then they will move forward throughout the West in one final effort to exterminate all of the Americans."

The prophet then paused for several seconds before saying firmly, "I assure you the extermination will not happen. The Lord does not intend for that army to reach these mountains. After much prayer and fasting, the First Presidency and the majority of the Quorum of the Twelve gathered this morning here at the Rexburg Temple, where the will of the Lord was made known to us in a clear manner. The time has come for the elders of this Church to rise up and defend this land. We are this continent's last hope for freedom and righteousness. Indeed, we are the world's last hope."

The prophet then rose to his full stature and said, "The land where the enemy now resides is where the Center Stake of Zion will be established and New Jerusalem will be built. In order for us to fulfill the Lord's prophecies, the enemy must be vanquished. As the Lord's earthly representative, I now call upon the righteous elders of this Church living in the Rocky Mountains to join together in what will be known as the Elders of Israel. Priesthood leaders, spread the word throughout your camps that every worthy elder is invited to be a part of this holy army. War is an ugly thing, but much like Captain Moroni in the Book of Mormon, I feel compelled that we must step forward to defend our families, our religion, and our God."

Doug's whole body was electrified. The time had arrived to battle the Coalition forces. He was raring to go.

Then the prophet said, "I know some of you high priests would like to join the army, but you will remain at the camps to maintain order and to protect the women and children if needed. Also, only young men who have been ordained to the office of elder in the Melchizedek Priesthood and who have received their temple endowment will be invited."

The prophet smiled. "I will leave the decision of which young men are eligible up to the local leaders, but I suspect there will be a flurry of ordinations and temple sessions taking place in the next couple of days."

That brought a chuckle from the group, and Doug knew his nephew David would be begging to join the army, even though he wasn't an elder yet. The prophet concluded by saying, "We ask that the elders in your group depart from your camp in one week, on the sacred day of April 6th. The church was restored on that date in 1830, and it will now forever be remembered as the day that the Elders of Israel marched forth to defend this land. Brethren, the Lord will be with you. This is His errand, and we will not fail."

Doug quickly rushed home from the meeting and burst through the door. "Everyone gather around," he called out. "I have important news."

Once everyone had crowded into the front room, Doug shared how the Coalition forces were gathering together as one army, and that in response, the prophet had called forth the Elders of Israel. He explained that the elders would depart in one week.

There were varied reactions from the group. It hadn't really occurred to most of them that the men in Manti would be called upon to fight in the war. There was actually a bit of a rebellious feeling in the room, and Doug was bothered by it. So he pointed at his brother-in-law across the room and said, "Tad, as an elder of Israel, will you follow the prophet and join the Lord's army?"

"Absolutely," Tad said forcefully. "It is the highest honor I could imagine."

His statement changed the attitude in the room, and optimism began to replace the initial worry. As expected, David soon went to his uncle and asked, "Am I old enough to join the army? I'll be 18 soon, and I had planned to be ordained an elder later this year."

Doug smiled. "You know, I pictured this exact conversation when I first heard the announcement in the temple. I feel good about it, but let's talk to your parents and see what they think."

As David told his parents about his wish to join the army, Emma stood with her arms crossed, fighting her emotions. His request had taken her by surprise. She was already dealing with the thought of Tad going away to fight a war, but she had been comforted by the thought that David would remain with her.

David looked anxiously at her. "Mom, I won't go if you don't feel right about it, but I really want to go!"

Emma felt a lump in her chest. She wanted to scream, "*Isn't one soldier per family enough?*" but she kept it inside, biting her lip.

Tad spoke up. "Honey, I feel calm about it, and I would really like to have David at my side. It would be good for both of us. We would watch out for each other."

Emma still felt like her heart was being squashed. "I need to think about it," she said. "I'll be back."

She grabbed her coat, marched out the door, and began walking slowly toward the temple a few blocks away.

"Heavenly Father, I need David to stay here," she cried out in the darkness. "Doug can't take care of everything by himself, and David would be able to shoulder most of the burdens that Tad carries. Having my husband leave is going to be hard enough. What more do you want from me?"

She sobbed quietly for a few minutes and soon reached the gate that surrounded the temple. The temple lights hadn't been turned on at night for several months to avoid using the electric generators and to keep the city hidden from the enemy, but on this moonlit night the building stood out like a mighty fortress.

"*You aren't the first person to sacrifice for the Lord's kingdom,*" the Spirit gently whispered. "*Every stone in this temple came forth through sacrifice.*"

The words struck Emma hard. "But David is so young! What if he's killed?"

"*Many young people have already given their lives in the Lord's service. Be assured that whether he lives or he dies, he will be on the Lord's errand.*"

The words of the Spirit were hardly comforting, but Emma sensed this was an argument she wasn't going to win. "Can't he just serve a mission once the war is over?" she asked. "Won't we need missionaries then, too?"

"David wants to serve the Lord, but he realizes the world has changed and he won't be given the chance to serve a full-time mission. You would have happily allowed him to serve a mission, yet now you want to deny him a similar experience. Serving in this army will allow him to grow in many ways and strengthen his testimony."

Emma literally shook with worry, but she now knew she couldn't deny David his wish. "I will let him go," she said.

At that moment, the Spirit filled her with a warmth that brought her to her knees.

"Thank thee, dear Father, for thy patience with me during my weak moments," she whispered before returning home to share the news with David.

Chapter 5

The next few days were filled with excitement as decisions were made about who was joining the army. In all, there were nearly 2,000 men who would be departing Manti and leaving on April 6th for Temple Square in Salt Lake, where they would receive further instructions from Church leaders.

The prophet followed up his earlier statement by announcing that a young man had to be 17 years old as of April 6th to be considered for the army, and 86 young men in Manti qualified, including David. Not surprisingly, every one of them volunteered to go. This led to a flurry of priesthood interviews, sustainings and Melchizedek Priesthood ordinations for these young men on the following Sunday.

David was ordained an elder by Tad that evening, and they were able to participate in one of three special temple sessions that had been arranged the following day to allow these newly ordained young men to receive their endowments. Tad and Emma accompanied David through the temple session, and as they stood together in the Celestial Room afterward, they clung to each other with tears in their eyes as they felt the Spirit testify of their eternal family bond. Their joy, however, was offset by the reality of their upcoming separation.

Soon the morning of April 6th arrived. The army had gathered on the southern slope of the temple hill where the Manti Pageant had been held for many years, and the rest of the community stood in the open grassy area below.

Thankfully, a deer-hunting rifle was still considered a necessity by most families in the Sanpete Valley, with some families having several high-quality rifles that they willingly donated to the cause. This allowed each soldier to have a rifle, along with a backpack full of supplies and ammunition. Their clothes and boots didn't really match like the uniforms of a typical army, but they still looked clean and professional.

Leah stood next to Emma on the grass below the soldiers and searched the group. "There they are!" she called out, spotting David and Tad partway up the slope. They waved to her as President Johnson moved forward to speak to the group at a makeshift pulpit near the bottom of the hill. Although it wasn't an official position, President Johnson had become the main spokesperson among the stake presidents and often made the final decision on crucial matters.

"These men who stand behind me are the next generation of valiant LDS men to defend our land," President Johnson said. "Many of us are descendants of faithful soldiers who served in World War I and World War II. We even have men among us today who served in the wars that followed. Now we are living through yet another war, known as World War III. Our prophet has asked these faithful men standing behind me to come forth during this devastating, difficult time to preserve the liberties of our land, and they are to be applauded for accepting the call."

A cheer rose up from the crowd, and the soldiers themselves joined in.

"Our United States government may no longer exist, but we are still the inhabitants of this great land," President Johnson continued. "We will yet raise up a great nation, built upon the principles that our Founding Fathers established. The principles in the Constitution were divinely inspired, and if necessary, we will defend those ideals with our lives."

The president paused as the crowd applauded loudly. He then added, "According to Brigham Young in the Journal of Discourses, the Prophet Joseph Smith said, 'The time will come when the destiny of the nation will hang upon a single thread. At that critical juncture, this people will step forth and save it from threatened destruction.' In that regard, I propose that we call this group of soldiers the Manti Men, in honor of the Minutemen from the Revolutionary War. The last time our land was invaded, the Minutemen played a key role in defeating the British. Let's make sure the Manti Men make a little history of their own."

The men on the hill let out a whoop, and then the whole crowd let out an even louder roar.

President Johnson let the cheering go on for nearly a minute, then he said, "The time has come for the soldiers to depart. Following a closing prayer, our soldiers are going to march to the base of the hill for final hugs and kisses good-bye, and then they'll proceed to the street and march toward Ephraim."

One of the other stake presidents gave a moving prayer pleading for the Lord's protection upon the men that brought tears to everyone's eyes, and then the soldiers moved down the slope. Emma rushed to Tad for a final, long kiss while David hugged Charles and Leah, then they came together for a big family hug.

"I love each of you so much," Tad said, wiping tears from his eyes. "We're going to make it through this. I just know it. Be good and pray for us."

Tad then put his hand on David's shoulder and they moved toward the street to join the other elders. When the men were all assembled in formation, each soldier held his rifle upright in front of him and looked straight ahead, not wanting to betray the emotions that were welling up inside each of them.

Their group's commander called out, "Forward march!" and 2,000 faithful sons of God began marching north past the Manti Cemetery. Charles and Leah rushed to the edge of the street. David was on the outer edge of the formation, and Leah reached out and touched his arm as he passed by them, before turning to hug Charles. "I'm going to miss them so much," she cried.

"So am I," Charles said, envious that he was too young to go. His uncle Doug was still going to be around, but the daily chores now fell to him, and Tad had told Charles he was counting on him to watch out for Emma and Leah. He felt a little overwhelmed, but he had recently been ordained a deacon by Tad, and he knew this was how he could honor his priesthood, too.

As the last of the soldiers passed by, the crowd instinctively moved into the road to watch them go. Many families, including the Norths, watched the army until they slipped out of sight over a ridge a couple of miles away.

Emma put her arms around her two children and steered them back toward the house. "Let's keep our heads up," she told them. "They are serving Heavenly Father, and that's what we'll do while they are gone."

Chapter 6

Emma had been surprised that Doug and Becky hadn't been in the crowd to bid the army farewell, but when she and the children arrived back at the house, Becky's agonized cries could be heard coming from one of the bedrooms. Emma rushed into the room to see Doug holding his wife's hand as she lay propped up on the bed.

"I think the baby is coming," he said.

"Why didn't you come get me?" Emma asked.

"We didn't want to interrupt you during the army's departure," he told her.

She gave him a scolding look. "Well, the men are on their way to Salt Lake, so let's get this baby here safely."

The Dalton children, Justin and Heather, were crouched in the hallway and acting a little frightened. "Let's go outside to play," Charles told them, and he and Leah took the younger pair for a walk around the block.

Emma had obviously given birth herself, but she didn't feel able to handle someone else's delivery on her own. "Doug, please go find Sister Codner. She lives on the next block. She's a midwife, and we could really use her help."

While they waited for Doug to return, Becky confided to Emma, "For some reason I'm feeling really nervous about this baby. What if something is wrong with it? I was exposed to that toxic cloud last fall, and it has just been a strange pregnancy."

Emma patted her shoulder. "Everything will be all right. The baby has really kicked a lot, so it certainly has plenty of energy."

"That's for sure," Becky said, "but I wish I could have gotten an ultrasound like I did with the other kids. That way I would at least know whether it was a boy or a girl!"

The contractions began to pick up again just as Doug and Sister Codner arrived a few minutes later. The midwife checked Becky carefully, then said, "I can feel the baby's head. It won't be long now."

After a few more pushes, the baby began to emerge, and a surprised gasp came from Sister Codner.

"What is it?" Doug asked.

"You have a son, but he's not doing well."

She quickly worked on the baby to clear his mouth and make sure he was breathing. Doug looked over her shoulder, then winced. "Oh no, he's missing an arm."

Becky let out a cry of alarm, but the midwife reassured her. "The baby looks all right, but yes, he's missing an arm and one of his legs looks underdeveloped."

Doug knelt down and comforted Becky. "We knew there was a chance of this. We'll make it through . . ."

Becky wiped back some tears and said, "What happened during the pregnancy doesn't matter now. Just let me hold my baby."

After a few more moments of checking the infant thoroughly, Sister Codner bundled him in a little blanket and gently placed him in Becky's arms. She cuddled him close and told him, "I wouldn't care if you didn't have any arms. You're my son."

At her words, the baby let out a cute little whimper, and then gave a smile that made them all chuckle.

Doug kneeled next to them. "If it was a boy, we had decided to name him Daniel after your father. Does that still sound good?"

"Yes, it does," Becky said, getting a little choked up as she thought of her parents, Daniel and Heather Brown, who had been killed during an earthquake near Las Vegas the previous year while traveling to Utah to be with Becky and her brother Josh.

Emma had quietly stood in the corner, a bit in shock, but now she came forward to look more closely at her new nephew. The little boy's eyes were filled with warmth, and Emma sensed a valiant spirit inside his frail body.

"He's beautiful," she said. "I would think that he must have a great purpose to come at this time in such a damaged little body."

At her words, a rush of the Spirit filled the room, and each one of them felt it. Doug blinked away a tear and said, "I completely agree."

Emma called for the children, and they soon gathered. They were naturally surprised by Daniel's condition, but they also were very accepting and each held him for a minute or two. Then they left the room as Becky attempted to have Daniel nurse, and he quickly took to that. She smiled and said, "It looks like he has a good appetite."

Within the hour, President Johnson came to the house. "I heard that Sister Codner had rushed over to see you, so I put two and two together that the baby must be on the way. How is everything?"

"The baby has some physical problems, but Sister Codner has been wonderful in making sure both Becky and Daniel are fine."

President Johnson took a moment to greet Becky and to see the baby, then he took Doug aside. "I know he seems healthy enough, but have you given him a priesthood blessing?"

Doug shook his head. "Not yet, but I would really like to. President, will you join me? I think I would like to go ahead and give him a name and a blessing."

The two men held little Daniel in their arms, and Doug began the blessing. As he did so, the Spirit touched Doug's mind and he was shown that Daniel had been a powerful defender of righteousness in the premortal world.

As he continued the blessing, Doug said, "My little Daniel, I sense that your years on earth won't be lengthy, but somehow during this time you will touch many people's lives before returning back to the Spirit World to continue your work in the Lord's kingdom. I bless you that throughout this time you will feel little pain, and that you will be a joy to everyone that knows you."

Doug closed the blessing, and then the men also gave Becky

a blessing that her body would recover quickly. By that evening, the household was running somewhat smoothly, and Becky and Daniel were able to get some rest.

Emma marveled that the baby truly didn't seem to be in any pain. Although Daniel's arrival was a challenge, Emma also considered it a blessing, because it helped keep her mind off Tad and David. She knew they would likely soon be facing their own difficulties very soon.

She also tried to keep her mind off Becky's brother Josh. The last time they had heard from him was nearly a month earlier when Elder Smith of the Twelve Apostles had forwarded Doug a message he had received from Josh. The message indicated that the Guatemalan group was doing well under the circumstances, but that they were unsure of their destination. They had crossed into Arizona and were trusting in the Lord. Emma couldn't quite fathom the difficulties that Josh and Kim were facing, but she knew they were fully capable of anything the Lord asked them to do.

Even so, Josh had asked the family to pray for the group, and so as Emma pondered their situation, she softly said, "Heavenly Father, thank thee for blessing us here at home, and please watch over Josh and Kim in their assignment to bring a remnant of thy people to build thy holy city."

Then she turned her attention to getting all of the children in the household ready for bed, although it was a challenge to keep them away from Daniel. The kids already loved him like he had been around forever.

Chapter 7

On the evening that Emma offered her prayer in his behalf, Josh was standing outside a Church meetinghouse that had been built in the small town of Polacca, Arizona. He gazed at the amazing scene around him as thousands of Guatemalan Saints were now safely camped within sight of the towering mesas on the lands of the Hopi tribe.

On the day of their group's arrival in Hopiland, Josh and Mathoni had briefly met with the Hopi leaders. The leaders had listened carefully to the group's situation, and in a show of brotherhood and compassion, they agreed to let the Guatemalan Saints stay on their lands.

Of course, there was also a hint of self-preservation in their decision. The Hopis were very wary of the Coalition forces that were living in the city of Page, and they reasoned the Guatemalan Saints would be helpful in case their lands were attacked.

However, the leaders felt confident they wouldn't ever be discovered, since the Coalition forces rarely traveled very far from the main highways, especially in this dry and barren land. None of the Hopis had received the chip, and were therefore invisible to the Coalition's chip scanners.

After the meeting, Josh and a tribal leader discussed the current situation in the United States. The leader told him, "Many years ago, long before these current troubles, one of our chiefs counseled us, 'Be self-sufficient so that you are not dependent upon others for survival. Don't rely on supermarkets for food and don't be entirely dependent on wages. What will happen to you if someday the white man's world collapses?' Now we see the wisdom in his words."

Josh thanked him for sharing that message, and as he pondered their discussion, it was obvious the Hopi and Mormon leaders were on the same wavelength.

As the Saints trickled into Polacca, the Hopis had been intrigued to see Mathoni slowly driving the group's bus behind the hundreds of wooden handcarts. The Hopis hadn't seen a motorized vehicle actually run since their own cars had run out of fuel shortly after the oil embargo the previous summer. Mathoni had parked it near the Polacca meetinghouse and then he and Josh began to empty the remaining bags of rice from inside it.

During the journey, the Guatemalans had called it the "bus from heaven" because it never seemed to run out of food or fuel, and it even got new tires every couple of weeks. The people didn't realize that Mathoni was a translated being who had no need to sleep and could travel across the land much more quickly than mortals could. In fact, he had spent several weeks before their departure from Guatemala stashing fuel containers, spare tires and additional food in caves throughout Mexico and into the United States. Then as the group began moving north through Mexico, Mathoni had retrieved the fuel and food from the closest hiding spots each night while everyone else was asleep.

Adding to the vehicle's intrigue was that Josh and Mathoni were the only people allowed inside the bus. They had decided it wasn't worth the risk of the Saints discovering the bus was carrying sacred metal plates that contained the history of past civilizations. Several months earlier Josh and Mathoni had retrieved the plates from an ancient cave in southern Mexico that had been sealed shut since Nephite times, and they planned to deliver the plates to the LDS Church president once New Jerusalem was firmly established. As the Lord's prophet, he would have the authority and power to translate the plates and then publish them for the Saints throughout the world to read.

But they knew they wouldn't be turning the plates over to the prophet in the foreseeable future, so a couple of days after arriving in Polacca, Josh woke up before sunrise and helped Mathoni unload the remaining food from the bus. Then Mathoni drove it to an isolated canyon and backed the bus up against a large rockslide. The two men got out and Mathoni locked the door.

"We can't just leave it here, can we?" Josh asked. "Somebody will surely find it and try to break in."

"You're right, "Mathoni said. "I'll take care of it. Go stand on the other side of the canyon."

After Josh was out of the way, Mathoni appeared to pray for a few moments, and then he pointed at a massive stone near the top of the rockslide. The stone rose into the air for a few seconds, then settled gently alongside the bus like a feather.

"Sheesh, this is like something out of Star Wars," Josh said under his breath. "Is Yoda around here somewhere?"

"Hey, I heard that," Mathoni called out. "Don't mock sacred things. Through the priesthood, even the rocks obey, and mountains shall move. But yes, as I watched Star Wars, it sure seemed like George Lucas was on the right track."

"Are you telling me that you—a translated being—actually sat in a theater and watched Star Wars?"

"Who didn't?" Mathoni responded slyly.

Mathoni started stacking boulders as if he were building a pyramid, and within a few minutes the bus was completely hidden under a stone structure that didn't actually touch the bus. It was a remarkable feat, and Josh could only admire the handiwork of his Nephite friend.

"Wow, those rocks look like they've been there for centuries," he said. "But if you can move mountains, how come you made me haul all of those heavy plates out of the cave by hand?"

Mathoni smiled. "Your mind never quits working, does it?"

"Not when it comes to sparing myself hours of back-breaking labor."

Mathoni turned serious. "I suppose the best way to explain it is that I'm authorized to use my priesthood as long as it doesn't interfere directly with man-made situations. Hiding the bus under rocks in this deserted canyon doesn't affect anything that a mortal has already done. But simply transporting the plates out of the cave, through the air, and into the bus to simply save you from an aching back wasn't authorized, since the prophets Mormon and Moroni had actually placed them in that cave through a lot of strenuous effort."

"That makes sense," Josh said. "Otherwise we mortals would let you guys do all of the work."

"That doesn't mean we can't help out in a pinch," Mathoni said. "Certainly you've heard about when David Whitmer was summoned by Joseph Smith to go to Harmony, Pennsylvania, where the prophet was translating the Book of Mormon. But David had decided he wasn't going to leave his farm until he had finished sowing his field. Do you remember the rest of the story?"

"I do. When David went to sow the field, it was already done. His sister then told him she had seen three men doing the work very rapidly the day before." Josh's eyes grew wide. "Was that you?"

Mathoni gave a little bow. "I can't take all of the credit, though. My two brethren did their fair share. But the point is that while we planted that field very quickly, we still had to do the manual labor just like David would have."

"I understand now," Josh said. "But since I didn't touch any of these rocks, someday you'll be able to move them and unbury the bus just as easily as you stacked them, right?"

Mathoni laughed. "Don't worry. I won't leave you on your own with this one."

The two men walked back to Polacca and arrived just as everyone was starting to awaken. A few people asked Josh where the bus was, and he could only say, "It was time for the bus to go back to heaven." The answer seemed to satisfy everyone, because in their eyes the bus had been a miracle in the first place.

⁂

Early that afternoon, Joseph Evehema came to the camp. He found Josh and said, "When we first met, I promised to have our leaders explain more about The Third Shaking and other prophecies our people have seen fulfilled. Would you and Brother Mathoni be able to join us this evening?"

"Absolutely," Josh said.

"Then come to the mesa tonight. The elders would also like to hear more about the Guatemalan group and your future plans."

That evening the two men found themselves meeting with several Hopi chiefs in a small ceremonial building on top of one of the mesas. There was a pleasant exchange of greetings, and Josh felt comfortable among them.

Their chairs were arranged in a circle, and Joseph introduced Josh to the group as a general authority in the LDS Church. He then invited Josh to explain why the Guatemalan people had traveled north. He took a few minutes talking about the devastation in Guatemala from Hurricane Barton the previous year, and how the storm had been the catalyst to gather together righteous people who were devoted to the Lord. It also prepared them for a greater purpose. When he told the Hopi leaders that the group was on its way to help build a holy city in Missouri, the men nodded and didn't seem surprised at all.

"That fits well with our prophecies," one of the men said. "We also expect to help build such a city in the east in preparation for the return of our White Brother."

"That's fascinating," Josh said. "Hopefully this means we're meant to work together. Please tell me more."

One Hopi was clearly the chief of the group, and the others looked toward him. After a moment he said, "I understand many of the Mormon beliefs, and as you know, many of our people are of your religion. They believe that our prophecies match well with your beliefs. Your people are preparing for the return of Jesus Christ, while my people await the return of Pahana, the White Brother. Many of the signs that Pahana told us to watch for have been fulfilled, and very few are left to occur."

"Will you share with me the signs that have been fulfilled?" Josh asked. He shot a quick glance at Mathoni, who seemed content with the direction the discussion was taking.

The chief nodded. "The White Brother gave us nine great signs to watch for that have been passed down among our people through the generations. We believe those signs have been fulfilled, and with their fulfillment we have entered the final days before Pahana's return. The first sign is the coming of the white-skinned men to this land, but who wouldn't live Pahana's teachings. These men would take the land that wasn't theirs, and they would strike against their enemies like thunder."

The chief paused, and Josh said, "That clearly sounds like the arrival of the Europeans in the Americas and their use of guns to subdue the inhabitants."

The chief merely nodded and continued, "The second sign is the coming of spinning wheels filled with voices, which we interpret as the white men bringing their families in wagons across the prairies."

"That makes sense," Josh said. "As the wagons passed by with the families inside, it must have sounded just like the sign describes. What is next?"

"The third sign is that a strange beast like a buffalo—but with great long horns—will overrun the land in large numbers. We interpret this sign as the coming of the white men's cattle."

"Ah yes, the good old Texas Longhorn," Josh said. "That's very interesting."

The chief continued, "The fourth sign is that the land will be crossed by snakes of iron."

Josh thought for a moment. "That sure sounds like the railroads to me."

The chief nodded once again and said, "The fifth sign is that the land will be crisscrossed by a giant spider's web."

That one didn't quite make sense to Josh, but Mathoni leaned over and whispered, "Think of the electric and telephone lines."

Josh smiled. "I once saw a photo of downtown Salt Lake City in the early 1900s. In the photo there were wires crossing everywhere along the streets, and even down the middle of the streets. Yes, a spider's web is a very good description of those wires."

The chief saw that Josh had figured out that sign and moved on. "The sixth sign is that the land shall be crisscrossed with rivers of stone that make pictures in the sun."

"That one is easy, especially when you think of the nation's freeway system," Josh said. "And I certainly have seen my share of mirages traveling along it. Wow, that's another simple but excellent description. What is the seventh sign?"

"It is that we would hear of the sea turning black, and many living things dying because of it."

Josh nodded. "When I was young I remember watching news stories about the Exxon Valdez tanker disaster that spilled oil along the Alaskan coast. It certainly fits, and I know it wasn't the first time there had been an oil spill. Very good."

The chief smiled a little and said, "I've seen the eighth sign with my own eyes. The sign says we would see many youth, both male and female, who would have long hair like my people, and would come and try to join the tribal nations and imitate our ways."

"That sounds like the hippie movement of the 1960s to me," Josh said. "I'm glad that era didn't last too long."

"We are too," the chief said, causing everyone to chuckle.

"So what is the ninth sign?" Josh asked.

"The ninth sign is that a dwelling-place in the heavens, above the earth, would fall with a great crash. It would appear as a blue star. Very soon after this sign, the great destructions would begin."

Josh was quiet for a moment. "I can't think of what the ninth sign could be. Have you interpreted it?"

"We have," the chief said. "It was the U.S. Space Station Skylab, which fell to Earth in 1979. According to many eyewitnesses, it appeared to be burning blue as it passed through the atmosphere."

"I had forgotten about that, but it fits perfectly," Josh said. "So where does that leave us?"

"Exactly where we are, living amid great destructions," the

chief said. "The White Brother also spoke of three great shakings that would take place before his return. He said the first two would happen sometime during the fulfillment of the nine signs. These two shakings would be as if the world was being shaken by one hand, but the third shaking would be as if the world was being shaken by two hands."

"What is your interpretation of the shakings?" Josh asked.

"We believe World War I was the First Shaking, with World War II being the Second Shaking. Sadly, it is clear that we are in the midst of the Third Shaking. But we now look forward to the dawn of the new era that is about to come forth when the shaking ends."

The men spoke for a few more minutes and promised to help each other's groups endure the coming days. Then Josh and Mathoni departed back to Polacca, walking quietly though the night as they pondered the evening's discussion.

"You didn't say much during our meeting," Josh finally said. "Are you all right?"

Mathoni winced a little. "The meeting brought back a lot of memories for me, both good and bad. I really had to bite my tongue, because I'm not allowed to share many other things that I know will happen soon. But I think we all know the world is drenched with evil right now, and the people of the United States are suffering the consequences of their wicked actions."

Josh was surprised at how beaten down his Nephite friend appeared. "Hey, what's going on?"

Mathoni sighed wearily. "I'm just feeling a lot of pain right now."

"What do you mean? I thought you couldn't feel pain."

Mathoni pointed to the backpack Josh was carrying. "You've got a Book of Mormon in there, don't you?"

Josh nodded and stopped to open up the backpack. He was learning to appreciate these quiet teaching moments with Mathoni. They were always unforgettable.

"Open up to Third Nephi 28:38 and read it aloud," Mathoni

said. "In this verse Mormon is writing specifically about my two brethren and myself."

Josh turned to the page and read, "*Therefore, that they might not taste of death there was a change wrought upon their bodies, that they might not suffer pain nor sorrow save it were for the sins of the world.*"

Mathoni began to sob, and Josh put his arm across Mathoni's shoulders as they walked. After a few minutes, Mathoni had worked the anguish out of his system. "Thank you for being understanding," he said. "The hardest part for me is that I witnessed those glorious years after the Savior's visit among my people, so I know how wonderful life can be when Saints work together in harmony. But right now the earth is so filled with wickedness that sometimes it just engulfs me."

"I can certainly understand why," Josh said. "It's a rough world out there."

"I'm sorry, I didn't mean to drag you down," Mathoni said. "Don't worry. I've seen what awaits you and the other faithful Saints, and you can't even begin to picture the glorious days that are coming. Your city will truly be a holy place, and I can't wait to see it. Let's just keep working hard to make sure these Saints are ready and worthy to be a part of it."

Chapter 8

Earlier that same day, Ken Turner lay flat on his back in the snow outside Temple Square in Salt Lake City. His hair felt like it was standing on end, and his hands were tingling.

There was a tall chainlink fence that surrounded the entire Church complex, including the Conference Center and the Church's office buildings to the east. Ken had just found out—the hard way—that the fence was electrified.

"Where are they getting their power from?" he shouted at a homeless man sleeping on the sidewalk. "The rest of this city is operating like it's the 1800s, yet the Church has electricity!"

With his legs still a little shaky from the jolt, Ken bitterly stood up and peered inside the gate. Temple Square's lawns were covered with snow, but there were several cleared sidewalks. Someone was obviously maintaining the place.

"Hey, if you can hear me, let me in," he called out. "I paid my tithing for years. That ought to buy me a few days of shelter. I'll even shovel the walks!"

Ken paused to listen, but his words were met with silence.

Finally he turned and started walking south toward his former office in the City Creek Center. His accounting firm had gone bankrupt several months earlier and he knew no one would be there, but at least it would get him out of the cold wind.

He reached his old office within a few minutes, and it looked like it had been rummaged though several times. Papers were scattered everywhere and his desk was tipped over. He leaned against the wall and hung his head, thinking about the past year of his life.

Not even a year earlier Ken had been the president of the accounting firm. The company had been doing so well that he had more money than he knew what to do with, and he held an important position in his LDS ward. Then the government introduced the chip. It was Ken's moment of decision, and he had failed miserably.

His failure wasn't obvious at first. In the first few months after he received the chip, the money continued to roll in. But then came the oil embargo that finished off the already-shaky U.S. economy, and daily life went into a nosedive.

Ken felt most guilty about what had happened to his family. He had worked hard to convince his wife and kids that the LDS members who had gone to the mountain camps were overreacting. Sure, the invitation had come from the prophet, but Ken convinced himself it was simply an invitation for those families who were struggling financially, rather than being an actual commandment. Either way, Ken had felt it was a foolish request by the prophet in many ways, particularly from an economic standpoint, since in Ken's mind the Church would be paying the expenses of everyone in the camps.

"The prophet seems determined to force the Church into bankruptcy," he had told his LDS employees. "Here we are, still working hard and paying our tithing, while those people in the mountains are living off of us."

Ken had actually succeeded in getting many of his employees—and even his wife Toni—to see his point of view, and his feeling toward the Church grew more bitter. He knew now that he'd been wrong, but it didn't take away the pain as he suddenly experienced a horrifying flashback. He covered his eyes with his hands as he recalled his family huddled in their home a few days after the economic collapse, hoping it would pass and that he could get back to work.

Then they heard on the radio that the Coalition forces had landed on both coasts. Toni became hysterical, and he finally agreed to take her and their two teenage children into the mountains to find an LDS camp. Ken had renounced his Church membership after receiving the chip, but he figured the leaders at the camp would be sympathetic and allow his family in.

Unfortunately for Ken's family, thousands of other LDS members throughout the Salt Lake area had also suddenly come to the conclusion that maybe the prophet had been right. They decided they could abandon their large homes and fancy gadgets after all—but it was too late.

As Ken steered the car that day from I-15 onto I-80 heading east toward Parley's Canyon, the Turners found themselves in a monstrous traffic jam. An hour later they had only traveled down the freeway about 200 yards, and people in the cars around them were getting irritated. The spirit of contention hung heavily over the entire area. Ken watched in shock as a family next to them literally bloodied each other in a violent fight inside their car as the father tried to calm his children down.

"Mindy and Bruce, make sure your doors are locked," Ken told his kids in the back seat. "Try to avoid eye contact with people in the other cars. They seem out of control."

Soon the cars started moving at ten miles an hour, and Ken was starting to feel optimistic. But then the gridlock set in again, and he wondered what the problem was.

"Oh no," Toni cried. "Look at that!"

Up ahead they could see two dozen young men approaching them in a line that stretched all the way across the freeway. Each one held a baseball bat and would jump onto the hood of a car before taking a big swing and smashing the windshield.

"Get down," Ken yelled. "Get as low as you can. Maybe they'll leave us alone!"

From the screams and sounds of shattering glass, the Turners knew the hoodlums were only moments away from reaching them. Suddenly two teenage hoodlums peered inside the car.

"Hey, check out that blonde," one said, pointing at Mindy. In a flash the men smashed the side window, popped the lock, and snatched Mindy before Ken or Bruce could even react.

"Dad, stop them!" Mindy screamed as they dragged her away. Ken and his son Bruce leapt out of the car to save her, but one of the thugs quickly turned and shouted, "Stay back!"

Bruce rushed forward anyway, and the thug flipped out a switchblade and plunged it into Bruce's chest. He slumped to the ground, and Ken instinctively turned to help him. In that brief moment, the thugs disappeared between two cars, still dragging a screaming Mindy. Ken tried to follow them, but one of the men put his hand over Mindy's mouth, and soon Ken wasn't able to track where they had gone.

After a short and frustrating search, Ken returned to Bruce's side. He did his best to save his son, but the blood was flowing too steadily, and he slipped away within a few minutes.

Toni had got out of the car and was now sitting on the roadway in shock.

"Somebody help us," Ken yelled. "My son has been killed."

But no one came toward him. In fact, most people were now abandoning their cars and fleeing from the freeway. In agony, Ken carried his son's body back to their car and placed it in the back seat. Then he went to check on Toni, who was crying uncontrollably. When Ken touched her shoulder, she slapped it away.

"Bruce is dead, Mindy is gone, and we have nothing left," Toni shouted at him. "How could you put us in this situation?"

Ken stammered for words. "This is a nightmare for everyone. What do you expect me to do?"

"Go find our daughter!"

Ken started to protest, because he sensed the odds of finding Mindy were slim, but he headed off in the direction he had last seen her, covering more than a mile as he called her name again and again. As the sun began to lower in the western sky, he started walking back to his car.

He found Toni sitting in the back seat now, with Bruce's head on her lap. She was beyond crying and was almost in a trancelike state. Ken tried to get her to talk, but she wouldn't even look at him. Finally he said, "We can't stay here. Let's walk home."

Toni's voice came out like a growl. "Do whatever you want. I'm staying right here with Bruce."

"Toni, he's dead! There's nothing more we can do here."

She simply said, "I wish I were dead, too."

Ken felt crushed inside. He threw his hands in the air and walked away. Even as he did it, he knew it was possibly the most cowardly thing a husband could do, but he didn't care anymore.

Ken returned to his house for two days, hoping that Mindy would somehow find her way home. He couldn't even bear to think of what she had gone through.

On the third day after Bruce's death, Ken went back to I-80 and located their car, but Toni was gone, as was Bruce's body. At that moment, Ken felt a crushing darkness surround him. For a moment he considered taking his own life, but he was too afraid of what awaited him on the other side of the veil. So he just started wandering through the neighborhoods of Sugarhouse looking for food, sleeping each night in an abandoned garage or basement.

He eventually moved toward the more upscale neighborhoods on the east bench, keeping to himself and avoiding some rough-looking men who seemed to be methodically looting the area. There weren't very many people left in the valley, and in everyone's panic they had left enough food behind that Ken wasn't starving to death. It was amazing how long he could make a box of Cheerios last.

As the winter snows began, he knew he had to find a permanent place to stay. To his delight he had come across an abandoned house with a basement pantry that contained a few dozen cases of Top Ramen noodles. He didn't have anything to heat the noodles with, but he would fill a pan with snow and then hold it against his body. The snow would eventually melt enough that he could put a packet of noodles in the water and soften them up a bit before adding the beef-flavored powder. He allowed himself two packets a day and figured the noodles would last him until spring.

Ken occasionally went outside and scanned the valley below him, but he didn't see another person for nearly four months.

He was fine with that. The guilt he felt over Mindy's abduction haunted him, because he was certain she had suffered greatly and then was killed. Combined with Bruce's death and Toni's mental breakdown, Ken felt worthless and ashamed, but also angry at the Church leaders. In his mind, the Church's invitation to go to the mountain camps hadn't been strong enough.

"They should have been more direct in their letter," he screamed at the walls. "They knew something was going to happen. Why didn't they make us leave?"

As spring approached, Ken sometimes saw smoke rising from near downtown Salt Lake. When he only had four packets of Top Ramen left, he decided to move in that direction. Soon he was standing outside Temple Square, looking in at the fenced Church complex.

And that's how Ken found himself flat on his back in the snow after the shock of his life.

Chapter 9

Ken stayed in his City Creek office for only a few minutes before catching sight of the smoke again through the window. It apparently was coming from the grounds of the State Capitol Building. He left his former office, walked around the Church complex, and slowly made his way up the hill toward the Capitol. His body was about to give out after his steady diet of noodles. For years he had tried to lose weight, and he laughed to himself that he had finally found a great diet solution.

As he reached the Capitol grounds, he was approached by a man in black clothing with a shaved head and a red goatee. The man waved a pistol at Ken and said, "Don't move another inch."

Ken put his hands in the air. "Hey, the way I feel right now, I wouldn't mind if you put a bullet through my heart."

The men stared at each other for a moment, then Ken dropped his hands and said, "Don't I know you?"

The man looked puzzled. "I don't think so."

"Yeah, I remember you," Ken said. "You're the CCA agent who came to my office and roughed up one of my employees last year."

The bald man shook his head. "That doesn't narrow it down very much. I used to work for the CCA, but I usually roughed up two or three people a day."

"So it *was* you!" Ken said, actually feeling slightly happy to see someone he knew, even if it was one of the government's hired goons. "Officer Fierce, isn't it?"

"Close. My name is Jonas Fernelius."

"That's right," Ken said more confidently. "Then maybe you

can answer a question. I've always wondered what happened to that employee you roughed up. You took him out of the office to retrieve some money, and I never saw either one of you again. His name was Tad North."

Jonas felt like he'd been punched in the stomach. Even hearing Tad's name made him furious. Jonas had driven Tad in his government-owned Ferrari to retrieve a $10,000 cash withdrawal that Tad had made under questionable circumstances. As they had taken the Springville exit and crossed the overpass, Jonas' world suddenly turned upside down.

In less than ten seconds, Tad had jumped out of the side door and Jonas had slammed on the brakes. A dump truck that was behind them had crushed the back end of the Ferrari, temporarily trapping Jonas inside. By the time he kicked the car door open, Tad had fled into a grove of trees west of the freeway.

Jonas had used a chip-tracking device to locate Tad hiding in a clump of bushes, but when he reached that area, Tad was nowhere to be seen. But the tracking device had kept blinking, and after a few minutes Jonas had found a tiny, bloody chip in the dirt. Tad had apparently cut the chip out of his own hand.

The government had issued an all-points bulletin seeking information on Tad's whereabouts, and a couple of days later his pants and shoes were found on the other side of Utah Lake in the locker room of Lincoln Point's community swimming pool.

Jonas knew Tad couldn't hide for long, but then came the big earthquake and the flooding of Utah Valley, and Tad's trail vanished. Not only was Tad never found, but neither was the $10,000 he had withdrawn.

The government assumed that Tad—and the money—had reached his Mormon relatives hiding in the mountains, and Jonas received the full brunt of his superiors' anger. He was soon fired from his job and was forced to make restitution for the damaged Ferrari and the $10,000. His savings was depleted, and his life was ruined. He had lived on the streets until this job as a security guard had come along.

Jonas shook his head, returning to the present and realizing he was still pointing a pistol at Ken, who was watching him curiously. "No one ever told you what happened to Tad?" Jonas asked.

"Nope. I figured you had retrieved the money and then killed him. It wasn't long after that when everything fell apart."

Jonas frowned. "Well, I wish I had killed him, but he escaped when we reached Springville."

"Tad escaped? Couldn't you track his chip?"

"He apparently cut it out himself," Jonas said. "The government made me suffer for his escape, and I'd rather not talk about it."

"That's fine with me," Ken said. "I'm just happy to be talking to another person. I've been on my own for the past few months. I'm sick of eating Top Ramen—and tired of talking to myself. I saw the smoke rising from this direction and hoped someone had organized some sort of government again so we could start getting back on our feet."

Jonas looked pleasantly surprised and lowered his pistol. "Well, you're in luck. A man named Larry Campbell has taken control of the Capitol Building, and I'm working as one of his bodyguards. He's extremely paranoid, and he suspects that anyone who wanders up here is some sort of Mormon spy."

"I admit I was once a Mormon, but not anymore," Ken said. "I've got a chip in my hand. Isn't that enough proof?"

Jonas nodded. "Yes, that should do. Plus, your bone-thin frame is plenty of proof."

"Good. I'm guessing your leader would be more than happy to have another follower who hates the Mormons."

"Absolutely," Jonas said. "Let me introduce you to Sherem."

"Sherem?"

"Oh, sorry. That's the name Larry likes to be called. He says it comes from the scriptures. He sees himself as some sort of savior. As long as he keeps me fed, I'll call him whatever he wants."

Jonas led Ken up the front steps of the Capitol and into the rotunda. There were a few containers of wheat and canned vegetables stacked in the hallway.

"It looks like you guys have been eating better than I have," Ken remarked.

Jonas laughed. "Yes, although we're starting to get low on supplies. Sherem's band of robbers made a haul a few months ago by killing off the Mormon families who stayed behind. The Mormons thought they could hide in their fancy homes, and most of them had enough food stored to live for quite a while. But their food couldn't protect them against Sherem's men."

The pair climbed a set of stairs and stood before the entrance to the Senate chambers, which had been converted into Sherem's living quarters. Jonas knocked loudly and called out, "Master Sherem, sorry to interrupt, but I have a new arrival for you to meet."

The men could hear some rapid shuffling, and within a minute two scantily-clad women opened the door and scurried past them. Soon Sherem also came to the door, pulling a colorful robe around himself.

"This had better be important," he said angrily.

Ken stepped forward and extended his hand. "I'm Ken Turner, and it's a great honor to meet you. It sounds like you're creating a new government, and I offer my assistance. I hear you aren't too fond of the Mormons. I was one myself once, but I blame them for the death of my children and would love to even the score."

Sherem looked him up and down, then said, "Yes, I think we can put you to work. We've noticed an increase of activity on Temple Square, as if they are preparing for something. I need you to watch that area closely and let me know of anything unusual."

"I would love to do that," Ken said. "I've already found out the hard way about their electric fence. That was quite a shock!"

Sherem took a closer look at Ken. "It looks like you could use a good meal before you go anywhere. Stay for dinner, and you can start your assignment tomorrow."

Ten minutes later Ken was sitting at Sherem's side at a large table that had once been used for committee meetings by Utah's state legislators. Several women hovered around them, bringing them each a tuna fish sandwich, a bowl of chicken noodle soup, and a small cup of soggy peas.

Sherem was somewhat apologetic. "Most of the Mormons apparently only stocked their pantries with these three canned items. But we have enough wheat to eat bread for quite a while!"

Ken smiled. "Believe me, this is a great feast."

They ate in silence for a few moments, then Ken said, "I must admit I'm curious about why you chose the name of Sherem. It comes from the Book of Mormon, correct?"

Sherem perked up. "You're right! I'm impressed."

"But I thought Sherem wasn't a good guy," Ken said hesitantly. "Didn't he get struck down by the Lord while confronting the prophet Jacob?"

Sherem laughed. "I can tell you are well-versed in Jacob's version of the story. But I see a different side of Sherem—a courageous man who stood up against the dominant religion. He opened the minds of the Nephite people to alternative ideas of happiness and pleasure. That is why I seek to emulate Sherem. I also provide an alternative to the dominant religion, and if I can bring joy and prosperity into the lives of my followers, I'll be satisfied. Just look around this valley. Where are the Mormons now? Hiding in caves and starving in the mountains? Yet here we are sitting in the State Capitol eating a fine meal. Surely we are living much better than they are—if they survived the winter."

Ken had to admit Sherem was very persuasive, but he wanted to know a little bit more about him.

"Based on what you have said, it sounds like you were also a Mormon once," Ken said carefully. "What caused you to eventually 'see the light' and become such a great leader?"

Sherem appreciated Ken's cautious wording. He had killed men who had been less worshipful toward him.

"Yes, I was raised in the Church and served in many callings," Sherem said. "I became a lawyer and was making a lot of money. I even lived in a spacious home that is higher on the hill than this place."

Ken was intrigued. It sounded like Larry "Sherem" Campbell had been on track for great things, both in and out of the Church. But he stayed silent, watching Larry's face twist in anger.

"Then came the trumped-up fraud charges that sent me to the state prison. I operated my law practice by the book, but the judge still felt I had violated the trust of my clients. I was willing to pay back every penny, but they wouldn't allow me to. The judge was a close friend of the prophet, and I still believe they had it in for me. So I started writing letters to the *Deseret News* pleading my case, and soon I was paroled. In some ways I think the justices were just tired of seeing my letters in the newspaper.

"Anyway, I was released to a halfway house in Sandy, and I started attending church there right before the Mormons were called to the mountain camps. After all that time in prison, the last thing I wanted to do was spend more time cooped up somewhere, so I stayed in the valley. Besides, when all the ward leaders left, I was a natural selection to be the new bishop."

Ken was incredulous. "That was only last year! You've gone from being a bishop to living in the Capitol? That's quite a climb."

"Well, I must admit the Church didn't consider me the bishop. I just took over the role. But it didn't last long, because the state claimed I had violated my parole and sent me back to prison. But I consider it an act of God that I was sent back there, because soon came the monstrous earthquake and the flooding of Utah Valley. As the water drained from Utah Lake into the narrow channel at the Point of the Mountain, it turned into a raging torrent fifty feet deep. The prison literally shook as the first wave slammed into it, and the water level didn't drop for several hours. Most of the inmates were locked in their cells at the time and didn't stand a chance as the flood waters rushed in."

"Then how did you survive?" Ken asked.

"I was one of the lucky ones who was getting some sunshine in the outside yard. As the flood hit, the guards took off and left us alone. The water pushed us against a brick building, and as the water got deeper, we just kept moving higher on the wall. Soon it was deep enough for us to reach the roof. As pieces of debris floated by, we would each grab a piece, and then we floated right over the prison fences."

"That's an amazing escape story," Ken said. "But didn't you just float all the way to the Great Salt Lake?"

Sherem smiled. "It was quite a ride, but the water began to spread throughout the valley, and we eventually could start wading. We fled into the Oquirrh Mountains near the Kennecott Copper Mine, and we hid there for several weeks as the national situation got worse. For some reason, the other inmates began to look up to me and obey me, especially after I changed my name to Sherem. We began to prey upon the people in the valley each night. Eventually there wasn't a government left to apprehend us, and we walked openly through the streets gaining followers, such as our friend Jonas here."

Jonas nodded from across the table. "When I first saw Sherem, I knew a powerful leader had risen up who would build a civilization destined to be greater than any in the past."

Sherem feigned modesty. "Jonas, you are too kind. But back to my story. One day I looked toward this end of the valley and the State Capitol was gleaming in the sun. It seemed to beckon to me. The building had suffered a bit of damage from the earthquakes, but for the most part, the expensive seismic retrofitting the state completed a few years ago has held up wonderfully. So now I have the biggest mansion in the valley, all thanks to the very state that put me in prison. Thank you, Utah!"

Ken smiled at Sherem's final comment. "So I suppose your army of men that have ransacked the valley's homes are the prisoners that escaped with you from prison?"

"Yes, some of the state's most notorious scoundrels now follow my orders. It's as if divine intervention has played a role in this."

"It certainly looks like it," Ken said. "I pledge my full support to you."

"Thank you," Sherem said, sincerely touched. "I have a feeling you will rise high in my kingdom."

As they returned to finishing their meal, Ken hid his emotions, but he was feeling extremely creeped out. He was smart enough to realize that Larry "Sherem" Campbell was a complete fraud, and a self-deluded one at that. It almost felt like he was sitting next to Satan himself. But as Jonas had mentioned earlier, as long as he had food in his belly other than Top Ramen, Ken could tolerate doing Sherem's bidding.

Chapter 10

Tad and David were toward the back of the group as the Manti Men marched down Salt Creek Canyon into the city of Nephi. They could see 2,000 righteous men winding down the canyon on their way to defend their freedom.

"This is an inspiring sight," Tad said. "I hope you always remember this scene."

David smiled back at him. "The part I'll remember the most is that my father was right beside me."

Tad bit his lip, surprised at the emotions his son's words had sparked. "I feel the same about you, son."

The Manti Men set up camp in Nephi outside the Wendy's Restaurant just west of the freeway. All of the lawns were still covered with snow, but the spacious parking lot had melted off nicely.

The next day they began walking north on I-15 toward Salt Lake. They expected it would take several days to cover the distance that once took less than two hours in a car.

As they passed through Spanish Fork and Springville, portions of the freeway were still covered with a thick layer of mud. It was strange for Tad to pass the flood-damaged areas he had traveled through after the earthquake. As they marched past West Mountain, Tad quietly pointed out to David the rocky ridge on the mountain's north end where he had been hiding from Officer Fernelius when the earthquake hit.

The group stopped one night to camp in a grove of trees west of what had been the Flying J Truck Stop in northern Springville, and Tad nearly had a panic attack as he relived one of the most terrifying moments of his life. He was within sight of the overpass where he had escaped from Officer Fernelius. He hoped to never see that evil man again.

Each of these landmarks meant nothing to the other men in the group—but they meant everything to Tad. He finally realized how often the Lord had watched over him. There were several times when he should have been killed. He bowed his head and softly said, "Thank you, Heavenly Father, for sparing my life."

Tad and David looked toward the Provo Temple, wishing there was time to pay a visit to Emma's parents, Mark and Michelle Dalton. They hadn't received any word from them since they had started their "guardian mission" the previous month, but Tad figured no news was good news. The previous year's flood had driven away all of the Provo residents who hadn't gone to the mountain camps, and the city appeared deserted.

"I doubt Grandpa Mark has used too many bullets," Tad told his son. "I don't see anybody."

"You're right, but I'm sure Grandma Michelle has kept him busy. I'll bet they've dusted the whole temple at least once," David said with a smile.

On the fourth day after leaving Manti, the group finally reached downtown Salt Lake. As they marched down the 600 South off-ramp and entered the city, they were amazed at how quiet it was. The snow helped mute any sounds, but each of the men were used to zooming down that off-ramp and into the congested traffic of a bustling metropolis. Now there wasn't even a car on the road.

There was quite a bit of earthquake-related damage throughout the downtown area, and so they walked carefully to avoid rubble and cracks in the road. They turned onto 300 West and walked past the abandoned Conquest Center, formerly known as the Energy Solutions Arena. A sign attached to the marquee in front of the building read:

Salt Lake Gladiatorzz vs.
Las Vegas Lounge Lizards
The battle begins tonight at 7 p.m.
Brought to you by Conquest --
Making your fantasies come true.

Tad pretended to ignore the sign, since no one else in the army besides David really knew much about Tad's previous obsession with the Gladiatorzz. David couldn't let it go, though. He elbowed his dad in the ribs. "Hey, maybe we could sneak down here tonight and you could put on your Tadinator outfit!"

"What a wise guy," Tad responded, playing along. "For your information, I actually attended that game. It was the night before the Great Storm, and the Gladiatorzz won in overtime, probably thanks to me."

"Hah! I'm sure you scared the team more than helped them."

Tad had to laugh. "You're probably right. What an idiot I was. But it looks like the Conquest league has bitten the dust."

The group turned toward Temple Square and soon reached the south side of the Main Street Plaza, where several men waited inside the fence to greet them. They had opened a gate in front of the Brigham Young statue and allowed the Manti Men to pass through.

"Everyone is in," one of the men at the gate called out. "Okay, stand back. We're turning the electric fence back on."

David thought it was interesting that they would have to put up an electric fence, but then it was as if his eyes adjusted, and on the sidewalk across from Temple Square there were more than a dozen vagrants watching them closely. He hadn't noticed them before, but they looked like wolves waiting to jump into a corral of sheep.

"Dad, look at those guys," he said.

"I see them," Tad responded. "Salt Lake certainly isn't as safe as it used to be."

One of the guides stood before them and said, "There are

elders already here who have gathered from other camps along the Wasatch Front. You are the last group to arrive, but we have set aside two floors here in the Joseph Smith Memorial Building for you to use as your sleeping quarters and to store your gear. We know you've been on your feet everyday since April 6th, so go ahead and get settled and cleaned up. There will be a meeting in the Tabernacle at 6 p.m., where you will receive more information about what lies ahead."

The Manti Men moved through the doors of the building, and inside they were greeted by elders from the other camps who shook their hands and welcomed them. There were groups from several areas, including Tooele, Huntsville, and the Heber Valley Camp, as well as men from a camp in Little Cottonwood Canyon.

"Hey Tad!" one of the men called out.

Tad turned around to see one of his friends from high school coming toward him. "Mike! It's good to see you. What group are you here with?"

"I'm part of the group that is living up at the Heber Valley Camp."

"Do you have a lot of elders here with you?"

Mike laughed. "Well, we had a dilemma. First of all, we were already at the camp when the big earthquake hit and caused the Jordanelle and Deer Creek dams to break. We were okay, but the floods pretty much wiped out any roads from Heber down to Provo, so we weren't sure what we were going to do when spring came."

"That's true," Tad said. "Your group was pretty isolated up in the mountains by the flood."

"Yes, but we had plenty of food and nice shelters, even though we received so much snow that it was higher than the roofs of the cabins. The road is impossible to even find right now, so only a few of us made it out to join the Elders of Israel—the ones who knew how to cross-country ski."

"You skied all the way here?" David asked.

"Well, all the way to Provo," Mike said. "Believe me, that was a wild trip down the mountainside, and Provo Canyon now has some wild jumps carved out by the water. So we had a good time, and it was some of the best powder I've ever seen."

"I'm glad you survived it! With that much snow up there, I guess you didn't have any worries about being attacked by the Coalition."

"Nope. We felt pretty secure," Mike said. "In fact, I'll be surprised if they even have the snow cleared off the road a month from now."

The two friends shook hands and agreed to talk later, and the Norths caught up with the rest of their group. When they reached their assigned floor, David slumped down. He suddenly felt more worn out than it should have, and he sensed they had plenty of walking still ahead of them.

That evening nearly 4,000 members of the Elders of Israel filed reverently into the Salt Lake Tabernacle. So far their journey had been fairly carefree. Their enemy was still hundreds of miles away, and they didn't quite understand what the Church's plans were. That was all about to change.

After beginning the meeting with a rousing version of "Called to Serve" that brought the Spirit strongly into the building, one of the elders offered a tender prayer. Then Elder Smith of the Quorum of the Twelve Apostles took the pulpit. He was known for his wit and candor, and the elders received a full dose of both during his powerful message.

After thanking the men for their willingness to leave their families and serve the Lord, Elder Smith said, "You are only one of several groups that are joining together to wage this fight against the enemy. There are also groups from the temple camps at Logan, Vernal, Boise, Billings, Cardston, and other sites that will join with you at Fort Bridger, several miles east of Evanston, Wyoming. This is not only a practical meetingplace for the various groups, it is also a symbolic gathering point. It is from that fort that a few dozen Mormon elders did their best to halt Johnston's Army in the 1850s.

Now, a few generations later, thousands of elders will meet there to prepare for the battle of their lives in defense of our liberty. You are members of this elite group, and through your prayers, faithfulness, and preparation, the Saints will prevail!"

The men applauded loudly, surprising even themselves. Everyone was now definitely fired up. Elder Smith closed his message with a short testimony that this was indeed the Lord's work, and then he answered a few questions.

Someone asked, "What's the situation in California? I have relatives there and I haven't heard from them."

Elder Smith said, "The good news is that the Saints who heeded the prophet's warning were safely tucked away in temple camps. Most of the California Saints have since moved to larger camps in Oregon and Idaho. You'll meet some of those elders at Fort Bridger.

"As for California itself, several situations such as the Coalition attack, the virus, the riots, and several large earthquakes have left it fairly uninhabitable. But we have small groups of priesthood brethren and their wives guarding the temples there, just like at the other temples."

Another elder asked, "What about this location? It's hard to believe that the Church would abandon Temple Square and all of its property here in Salt Lake."

"You're right, "Elder Smith said. "There will come a time when Salt Lake will once again be a thriving city filled with Saints. But first we need to rid the land of the Coalition forces, and then establish New Jerusalem. Once the center stake is in place, other cities will begin to blossom again across the continent—and Salt Lake will prosper like it never has before.

"This city will always be an important part of the Lord's kingdom, but the headquarters of the Church will be permanently moved to New Jerusalem. I know some people questioned why the Church spent so much effort and money on the City Creek Center and other projects if we were just going to move. But once the cleansing of the nation is complete, the Saints will return here and create a Zion society—with the benefit that the buildings will already be in place."

The apostle took a few more questions along the same lines before saying, "To help you understand the worldwide scope of establishing Zion, let me tell you about one special group that hopefully you will all eventually get to meet. At this moment, there are several thousand Saints making their way northward from Guatemala. They have recently entered the boundaries of the United States and are being watched over until the time comes for them to assist in the building of Zion.

"The group is being led by a general authority, and their arrival will help fulfill several of the great prophecies in the Book of Mormon, including promises made by the Savior himself to their ancestors during his visit to them following his resurrection. You brethren will witness with your own eyes the fulfillment of the promise that the tribes of Ephraim and Manasseh will work together to build New Jerusalem. Brethren, the Lord always fulfills his promises, even in ways we never would have imagined."

After the meeting, Tad and David waited to speak with Elder Smith to confirm whether the Guatemalan group he had mentioned was the one being led by Josh Brown. They introduced themselves to the apostle and thanked him for his talk.

Then Tad said, "Elder Josh Brown is a close friend of mine, and we're essentially in-laws, but he and Kim have been out of contact with us for a while. Is he the general authority that is leading the Guatemalan group?"

Elder Smith smiled. "He is. I'm in contact with Elder Brown every few days, and that group is definitely being watched over. I had the privilege of visiting the group in Guatemala last year before the hurricane hit the area, and I felt a tremendous sense of purpose and righteousness among those Saints."

"Will they join us soon?" David asked.

"They've made it through the hardest part—the journey

through Mexico and to their present location. But they'll likely stay there until it is time to join the rest of the Saints—which will be after the land of Zion is safe again."

"I'm so relieved to hear that," Tad said. "Well, the next time you're in contact with Josh, let him know that David and I are doing our part for the cause."

"I certainly will." Then the apostle put his hand on David's shoulder. "You take care of your dad, okay?"

"You can count on it, Elder Smith."

The apostle smiled at both of them, and then moved on to talk with other elders. But Tad and David were feeling sky-high, and the Spirit burned deeply in David's chest that Elder Smith was a chosen servant of the Lord, and the words he had spoken that night would be fulfilled.

Tad looked over at his son through misty eyes. "That's an awesome feeling, isn't it? I'm feeling it, too."

Chapter 11

Josh and Kim were eating a simple lunch in Polacca that same day with several Guatemalan and Hopi families. The two groups had mingled well together, and the Browns had been intrigued by the similarities of the two cultures. Many of the Saints from both groups commented that they felt like they had found long-lost cousins, and judging by the way they immediately accepted each other, it truly seemed like a big family reunion.

Kim had been fascinated how the Hopis' whole existence revolved around corn. They firmly believed that "Corn is life" and from what Kim had seen, they were absolutely right. Before coming to Hopiland, Kim hadn't really thought there was more than one kind of corn. But the Hopis had several different kinds of corn, coming in a variety of colors.

Kim watched with delight as two beautiful Hopi girls each operated their own ancient grinding stone. Their jet-black hair and olive skin radiated a purity and goodness that she had rarely seen among young people.

As the girls worked, their grandmother sat nearby and sang a traditional song that helped the girls keep pace as they repeatedly pushed a large flat stone back and forth, turning dried corn kernels into corn meal that could be used to cook more than 30 different dishes.

Kim greatly admired the special unity that Hopi mothers and daughters showed. One family had shown her their treasured cooking stone that had been passed down for many generations from mother to daughter. Their culture had developed more than

1,000 years ago, and little had changed over the centuries. But there was a strong sense of peace and security in their villages on the mesas.

"You two are adorable," Kim told the girls, who smiled and kept right on working.

Just then, Joseph Evehema came running toward them with a worried look. "Elder Brown, our scouts have big news," he said breathlessly. "The Coalition forces at Page are starting to move out. From what we could tell, they are moving east."

Josh nodded, not surprised. "That's what the Church leaders said would happen. It sounds like all of the remaining Coalition forces are gathering in Kansas City in preparation for one giant push into the Rocky Mountains."

"I hope the Church leaders have prepared the Saints to defend themselves," Joseph said.

"They have," Josh said. "We're hoping the Coalition won't know what hit them. I want to see these soldiers, though. What freeway will they be traveling?"

"We expect them to go down to Flagstaff and then turn onto I-40. That means they'll be passing by several miles south of here."

"Do you have a pair of horses we could use?" Josh asked. "I want to get an estimate of how many soldiers are in this group so I can let the Church leaders know."

Kim didn't like the sound of their plan. "Where's Brother Mathoni?" she asked. "Is he going with you?"

She didn't know Mathoni's true nature, but she had noticed that nothing bad seemed to happen if he was along on an expedition, and she considered him Josh's good-luck charm.

"Sorry, dear, but I haven't seen him, and we better be on our way," he said, giving her a kiss. "We'll be back this evening."

Josh did actually know where Mathoni was, but he had to keep it to himself. The Nephite had been summoned to Rexburg for an update on the war and how to best help the Guatemalan group. At first, it had been mind-boggling for Josh to realize how in touch Mathoni was with the modern apostles, but now it seemed natural that he would be working with the priesthood leaders of this dispensation. His whole purpose was to assist the Savior in bringing souls to Christ, and that sometimes included helping out behind the scenes of the latter-day Church.

Soon Joseph and Josh were on horseback galloping to I-40. "We should be way ahead of them," Joseph said, "but I'd like to get safely hidden, since they'll probably have their own spies."

By mid-afternoon they were hidden behind a rock outcropping about 300 yards from the freeway. They had left the horses in a grove about a quarter mile away. Sure enough, within a half hour came a small group of Coalition soldiers. They would occasionally check out some thickets or behind a hill, but it was clear that they didn't expect to find any opposition—or even any people out in the middle of the desert. This group passed by their outcropping without even looking twice at it.

After another half hour, a large contingent of soldiers came over the horizon. They were all on foot.

"Where are their tanks?" Josh asked. "I saw several of them parked on the streets in Page."

"I think they have used up all of their fuel," Joseph said. "Our scouts said the soldiers drove the tanks to Page, but in their boredom they drove them in the nearby hills and wasted all of the fuel."

Josh shook his head. "They probably thought they would have an endless supply, but according to the Church reports, neither China nor Russia has sent reinforcements of any kind. In fact, those two countries supposedly aren't getting along right now."

Joseph pondered Josh's words. "That is good news for us, right? Our elders just have to conquer the remaining soldiers, and then the land will be ours again."

"That's right," Josh said, "but it isn't going to be easy."

The men lapsed into silence as they began counting members of the army. It took almost twenty minutes for the rows of soldiers to pass by.

"It's a rough count," Josh said, "but I'd say there were at least 7,000 soldiers. Let's hope the Elders of Israel can handle them."

✣ ✣ ✣

Joseph and Josh returned after dark to Polacca, and they reported to the people what they had seen.

"What exactly does this mean?" one of the men called out.

"According to the Church reports, these soldiers are on their way to Kansas City, Missouri," Josh told him. "Once they are there, the final battle won't be far off. Meanwhile, our elders are organizing themselves to defend our freedoms. All we can do is wait to hear how the battle turns out."

That night Josh and Kim lay awake past midnight talking softly about the upcoming conflict and what it would mean for their family members. Communication between Church groups was extremely limited, but Doug had received permission to send a message to Josh a few days earlier that had updated them on the situation in Manti. It had made Josh want to lead the group all the way to Utah, but the snow still would have been a huge obstacle—plus the Spirit whispered to him that the Guatemalan Saints were right where they needed to be.

"I know that we are needed here," Kim said, "but sometimes I wish we could be there for Becky and Emma. I really miss them. That must be so hard for Becky to handle those little kids in those circumstances, and Emma has both a husband and a son in the Elders of Israel."

Josh gave her a hug. "I'm sure they wish you were there, too. But I have a feeling we'll be seeing them sooner than we expect."

CHAPTER 12

On the morning following Elder Smith's inspiring speech in the Salt Lake Tabernacle, the Manti Men joined the soldiers from the other camps as they departed Temple Square through a gate on North Temple Street. They marched west before turning onto 300 West and passing the abandoned Crown Burger restaurant on the corner. Tad and David glanced at each other, knowing they both were longing for one more meal there—or at least a side order of French fries and sauce. But they shook off their yearnings for fast food and continued toward the 600 North on-ramp to I-15.

Their fastest route to Fort Bridger in southwestern Wyoming would have been on I-80 through Parley's Canyon, but the snarled traffic jam of the previous fall had never been cleared, and thousands of cars still clogged the freeway. Scenes of carnage and murder had taken place throughout the canyon all the way to Park City.

There were also reports that many escaped convicts were now living in the canyon, working under the direction of a madman who lived in the State Capitol. The Elders of Israel could likely handle them if there was a battle, but the Church leaders felt it was an unnecessary risk. Every soldier would likely be needed in the fight against the Coalition forces, so it was decided that the Elders of Israel would take a slightly longer march and completely avoid I-80.

Instead, the soldiers would march toward Ogden and then take I-84 through Ogden Canyon before reaching I-80 past Morgan and traveling to join thousands of other soldiers at Fort Bridger.

Not far from the 600 North on-ramp, Ken and Jonas hid inside an abandoned home, peeking their heads above a window sill as they watched the soldiers pass by. Suddenly Ken whispered, "Hand me the binoculars!"

He focused his gaze on a man right in front of them. The soldiers had stopped in the middle of the street to get a drink of water before getting onto I-15. The man was leaning against a handcart that carried five-gallon water jugs, and Ken was willing to bet his life that he was looking at his former employee Tad North.

Ken handed the binoculars to Jonas. "Look at the guy leaning on the cart. Isn't that Tad North?'

Jonas studied the man for a moment, then cursed as he reached for his pistol. "That's him. I want to shoot him right now."

Ken grabbed his arm, afraid he might actually do it. "Don't be a fool. It would be suicide with all of these soldiers around, and I don't feel like dying today." He took the binoculars back. "Hey, the guy he's talking to has a bandana on his head that says, 'Manti Men' across it. I wonder . . ."

Ken had been to Manti several times to watch the Manti Pageant with his ward's youth groups, and he had even attended a few temple weddings there. He vaguely remembered people even predicting that Manti would someday be a place of refuge.

"This sounds too easy," Ken said, "but I have an idea that might be as satisfying as shooting Tad—I know where his wife and kids are. We could go take care of them, and then bring back all of their food."

Jonas rubbed his hands together. "Yeah, that would be revenge at its best. Where are they?"

"Manti. It's a small town tucked away in the mountains about 100 miles away, but I'll bet you anything that's where the families of these guys are. If we can convince Sherem to send his army of criminals down there, we could wipe out everyone left in town."

Ken and Jonas quietly moved out the back door of the house

away from the army and hurried back to the State Capitol. As they approached the building, they could hear Sherem shouting at someone. Jonas slipped inside and then motioned for Ken to follow him into a side room. "When Sherem's in this kind of mood, it's best to just stay clear of him," Jonas said.

They left the door open a crack, and they could see Sherem facing a long-haired man. His voice got louder and higher. "I told you to slip inside Temple Square when the gate was open. No one would have seen you. I ought to have you killed for this!"

Then they watched Sherem forcefully punch the man in the jaw, causing him to stagger. "I'm sorry, Master Sherem. There were soldiers coming out of the gate the whole time. They would've seen me for sure."

Sherem threw his hands in the air. "What a weak-minded idiot you are! You disgust me. I gave you one simple assignment and you didn't come close to completing it. Get out of here and don't ever come back."

The man quickly moved toward the open door, holding his jaw and muttering under his breath. Sherem watched him depart, then turned and walked up one of the elegant staircases.

Jonas and Ken looked at each other with wide eyes. "How about we stay here until he cools down a little?" Jonas asked.

Ken gave a little smile. "That sounds good to me."

After twenty minutes, the men left the room and found Sherem upstairs enjoying a breakfast of canned pears and wheat bread. He welcomed them graciously as if everything in his world was wonderful, with no hint of his recent confrontation.

Ken bowed respectfully toward him, then said, "I have great news. The Mormon army has left the valley and the threat of them bothering us is over. But more importantly for us, I believe that thousands of Mormon women and children are living near the Manti Temple."

Sherem looked at him strangely. "Why should I care about some Mormons living in Manti? They are no threat to us."

"There are plenty of reasons," Ken said hastily. "First of all, they probably have a lot of food stored there. Also, if we don't eliminate them, their children might grow up and try to reclaim Salt Lake. They would be a threat to your kingdom. But your army could easily get rid of them all and bring the food back with them."

Sherem finally appeared to be interested in Ken's words. "That's true, but what proof do you have that anyone is living there? I'm hesitant to send my men there if Manti is just an abandoned, frozen wasteland like the rest of the cities down south."

"Well, as the Mormon army was leaving, I saw a man wearing a headband that said 'Manti Men' and he was talking to a former employee of mine named Tad North who disappeared last year, but he's now part of that army. It all fits together that they left their families in Manti."

Sherem's expression changed dramatically. "Did you say Tad North? The one who lived in Sandy?"

"Yes, that's where he lived."

Sherem visibly shook. "I can't believe this. I put my strongest curse on him. How is he still alive?"

Ken and Jonas looked at each other in confusion. "I don't understand," Jonas said. "When would you have ever met Tad?"

"It was last year when I took over as bishop in Sandy after the other leaders had left. I guess his family had gone to the mountains without him, but Tad continued to attend our ward. On the day I stood before the congregation for the first time as bishop, a voice distinctly told me, 'Tad North must serve as your first counselor.' I saw him sitting in the congregation, but when I issued the call from the pulpit, Tad laughed at me and left the building. I never saw him again, but I felt prompted to pronounce a curse upon him that would end his life."

"Well, so far your curse hasn't worked," Jonas said. Then realizing who he was talking to, he hastily added, "But I'm sure it will take effect any moment now! He did look a little tired when we saw him earlier."

Sherem gave him an angry glance. "Watch your mouth, unless you want to receive a curse as well." He pondered quietly for a moment. "But possibly this is all related. Maybe the curse is actually meant for Tad's wife and children."

"I'm sure that's the answer," Ken said, trying to divert attention from Jonas.

Sherem rose from the table, looking regal yet sinister. "Yes, the curse is going to be fulfilled even more profoundly than I could have ever dreamed! But first I want to know how many people are actually there. I don't want to send my entire army if just a few men could do the job."

"That makes sense," Ken said, trying to keep Sherem happy. "We could first send a spy into Manti pretending to be a Mormon and discover where their food is hidden before we kill them all."

"That is a great idea," Sherem said. "Ken, as a former Mormon, you are the perfect man for the job!"

Ken smiled weakly. "Thank you for your faith in me, but there's a small problem. Tad's wife Emma knows me and would recognize me immediately. I'm sure she blames me for Tad receiving the chip, and I don't think I could convince her I was sincere."

Before Sherem could respond, Jonas said, "I'll go. I grew up around Mormons and I know enough of their beliefs that I shouldn't have a problem fitting in."

"Very good," Sherem said. "But Ken, you could take a few hundred of my men to Nephi and wait for a signal from Jonas. He could let you know when to begin the attack."

"Yes, let's do it," Ken said.

Sherem raised both hands. "But I do have one request. Certainly kill everyone else, but bring back Emma North and her children alive. I feel it is my duty to personally make sure the curse is fulfilled. We can execute them here."

"It would be my pleasure," Ken said. Deep in his heart, he knew he had just taken another step toward eternal destruction, but at that moment he didn't care. He could tell that Sherem was impressed with him, and he knew he could rise quickly in this new kingdom. Besides, if the raid went smoothly, he might even bring back a couple of the prettiest Mormon girls for himself.

That night Ken and Jonas worked out more of the details of their attack. Sherem had already summoned hundreds of his most vicious men, and they would leave for Nephi in the morning. Once there, Jonas would travel through Salt Creek Canyon to Manti.

"There will probably be guards somewhere in the canyon," Ken said. "Just tell them you are a friend of Tad North and that you are seeking forgiveness for ever leaving the Church."

"Do you really think they will believe me?" Jonas asked.

Ken look at his friend's right hand. "If they don't believe you, offer to let them cut the chip out of your hand. That should convince them."

Jonas winced. "I hope it doesn't come to that."

CHAPTER 13

Less than a week later, Sherem's band of wicked warriors had settled into the same Wendy's parking lot in Nephi where the Elders of Israel had camped earlier that month. Sherem had stayed back at the Capitol "to keep an eye on things" and he had put Ken in charge of the army. Some of the criminals resented that a little bit, but so far they had stayed in line, hoping for a nice reward of food and plunder, with some murder mixed in.

Jonas was feeling unexpectedly nervous as he and Ken walked to the mouth of Salt Creek Canyon the following morning.

"Just stay on the paved road and you'll be fine," Ken said. "Like we discussed, the Mormons will certainly have some guards stationed somewhere along the way. Just pretend you are a friend of Tad North's like we talked about and they'll probably take you all the way to Manti."

The snow had melted off most spots of the road, but there was still a substantial amount of snow in spots, and judging by the boot marks in those spots, there had indeed been a large amount of men passing through the canyon recently. "It had to be the Manti Men," he said to himself.

By mid-afternoon, Jonas had walked several miles without seeing anyone, but he soon approached a wider spot in the canyon that had a few buildings. He saw a sign that pointed to something called the Nebo Loop Scenic Byway. It was a paved road, too, and suddenly he was confused about which direction to go.

As he stood in the middle of the road, a man with blonde hair and a mustache stepped onto the pavement a few yards ahead of him. "Stay where you are," the man said, "and keep your hands where I can see them."

Jonas immediately noticed the rifle in the man's hand and put his hands in the air. The man moved within twenty feet and asked, "What's the password?"

Jonas was momentarily speechless and finally just shrugged. "I don't know. I'm just hoping to find a group of Mormons. I was once a Mormon, but I went astray. I've been living in Salt Lake for the past few months and have realized the error of my ways. I've repented and want to return to the Church."

The guard frowned. "You're hardly the first person to tell me that. Lots of people have a change of heart because of an empty stomach. What else can you tell me? Do you know anyone who might be here?"

Jonas swallowed hard. "I'm actually a good friend of Tad North. I figured he would be in this camp."

The guard's expression changed quickly to a smile. "Yes, that name rings a bell. Tad has gone to help fight the enemy, but his wife Emma is in Manti. I'm actually Emma's cousin, Richard Dalton."

"Wow, that's wonderful," Jonas said. "I'm so grateful to see a friendly face again. There's a madman running Salt Lake now, and it's frightening to live there."

"That's what we have heard," Richard said. "But it sounds like our army made it through Salt Lake without any problems."

Jonas smiled. "Yes, I actually saw the army as they were heading out of town, and I saw some 'Manti Men' headbands. That's why I came this direction in hopes the families of the men were here. I wish I had known Tad was with them. Well, I guess now I'll go find Emma and see if I can help out their family."

"That would be fine, but I need to give you a pass that shows I let you through."

Richard pulled out a red card from his pocket and began writing on it. "What's your last name?"

Jonas figured there wasn't any reason to tell the truth at this point. "Ferguson. Jonas Ferguson from Salt Lake."

Richard completed the card and handed it to him, and the men shook hands. "Thanks so much," Jonas said. "You've been an invaluable help."

Jonas turned to start walking up the road when Richard said, "Hey, I'll be trading my shift with the other guard in a few minutes. I've been wanting to get back to Manti to see my wife and kids, so if you want, I'll let you ride with me back up the canyon."

"Are you sure?" Jonas asked. "If you're supposed to stay here on guard I can just keep walking."

"It will be fine," Richard said. "It has been really slow all winter, with just a few stragglers coming up the canyon once in a while. By the way, did you see anything happening in Nephi?"

Jonas shrugged. "Nope. I didn't see a soul after I left Payson."

Richard took a moment to go into the main building and turn over his duties to his partner. As Jonas waited for him, he had mixed emotions. He had helped devise Sherem's plan and still felt that killing Tad's family would be justified, but he had a small problem—he hated lying, especially to good people. He blamed this trait on Sister Hall, a large, slightly surly woman who had taught the youth Bible class in his Protestant church. His parents had forced him to attend church until he was 14, and at times, Sister Hall's voice still bounced around in his mind.

Jonas had heard her voice every once in a while during his job as a CCA enforcement officer. He had roughed up a lot of people while performing his duties, but sometimes when he was about to go too far, he would hear Sister Hall's voice say something like, "*Blessed are the peacemakers.*" It drove him nuts, but it probably saved him from becoming like the criminals in Sherem's army who had seemingly lost their humanity.

Richard soon appeared with two horses he had retrieved from a nearby barn. "Have you ever ridden a horse?" he asked.

Jonas smiled, finally getting a chance to tell the truth. "It's been a while, but I should do okay."

They made good time on the horses, reaching the town of Moroni before dark, where several LDS families were living. Richard stopped at the home of an acquaintance, and the family made Jonas feel right at home, even feeding him a nice turkey dinner. The men departed again early in the morning, arriving in Manti around noon.

Richard went straight to the home where the Daltons and Norths were living. He told Jonas to stay with the horses on the street, then he knocked on the front door. Emma opened it up to see her cousin standing there. "Richard, what a surprise! It's good to see you. Come on in."

Richard gave her a quick hug then said, "I'd like to stay, but I really want to go see Melanie and the kids before I have to head back to the guard station. However, I have a man here who is a friend of Tad's. It sounds like he was off-track for a while, but he seems sincere about getting back into the Church."

Emma looked past Richard to see Jonas standing with the horses. "Hmm. You're sure he can be trusted?"

"I've spent the past day with him, and he seems like a really nice guy. Like I said, he claims to be a good friend of Tad's."

Emma hesitated. "I can't remember Tad ever mentioning anyone named Jonas, but maybe they were friends at work."

She walked with Richard out to the horses and shook hands with Jonas. "Hello, I'm Emma Dalton."

"It's a pleasure to finally meet you, " Jonas said. "Tad was always talking about you."

Emma smiled, but was still unsure. "Forgive me for saying this, but I don't remember Tad ever mentioning you."

Jonas inwardly gave a sigh of relief. He realized that even if Tad had ever told Emma about his escape, he doubted Tad ever knew him by any name other than Officer Fernelius.

"I'm not surprised. I actually worked as part of the City Creek Center's security team," Jonas said, stretching the truth. "Tad and I would have lunch together once in a while, and I was really impressed with him. I even gave him a ride once."

Emma smiled. "That was very nice of you. We were a one-car family, so I'm sure he appreciated it."

Richard waved his hand. "Well, I'll let you two get acquainted. I'm off to see my family. I'll be heading back to the guard station in the morning, but let me know if you need anything."

They watched Richard lead the horses down the block to his home, and Jonas asked, "How come Richard didn't go with the army? He certainly looks like he could handle it."

"Everyone in the army is an elder. Since Richard once served in a bishopric and was a ordained a high priest, he couldn't go. He was disappointed, but he sure makes an excellent guard."

Emma's explanation about elders and high priests made no sense to Jonas, but he nodded. "I'm just grateful he believed me and brought me here."

Jonas couldn't believe how smoothly the plan was going. He would stay throughout the evening and gather more information about the Mormons, then he would steal one of Richard's horses and hurry back to Nephi with the news that there were thousands of Mormons awaiting them. Within a couple of days all of the people in the valley would be dead, and Emma herself would be tied up and on her way to the State Capitol to meet a cruel end.

Emma led Jonas inside the home, where he met Doug and Becky, and they seemed like really nice people. They asked him a lot of questions about Salt Lake and the living conditions there, and they talked like old friends. He had to admit that his conscience was being pricked just a little bit. These people were treating him so well, and they readily believed everything he told them. To his dismay, he was actually starting to like them. Did these people deserve to die?

As they ate dinner, Emma asked him, "Since you worked in the same building as Tad, did you know his boss Ken Turner?"

"I did. In fact, it was because of him I got misled for a while," Jonas said. "I realize now that Ken was wrong, but he has a powerful personality and can convince you his ideas are right."

Emma bristled a little. "That's what happened to Tad. Ken talked him into getting the chip and soon everything went downhill for us. That's when I finally had to leave and move in with my parents in Springville." Suddenly Emma's eyes grew wide. "You don't still have the chip, do you?"

"Actually I do."

Doug sat up straight. "That could be a problem. We really like you, Jonas, but if you're going to stay here, you need to remove it. We can't risk the enemy detecting us because of your chip."

Jonas pretended to be relieved. "I'm glad you mentioned that. I have wanted to remove it for a long time, but I don't have the courage to do it myself."

"We can help you with that," Doug said. "We've done it in the past. Of course, no one has had the chip removed in quite the way that Tad's was."

"What happened with him?" Jonas was now really curious.

"Well, maybe you didn't know, but Tad had some troubles with the Chip Compliance Agency, and they actually took him into custody. One of the CCA's officers was driving him to Springville when he managed to escape into a grove of trees. Tad said the officer was going to track him down and kill him, so he cut the chip out of his own hand with a piece of glass. He still has an ugly scar."

Jonas felt a rush of anger to hear his own folly described, but he quickly covered his emotions by saying, "That's incredible! Tad actually got away? That officer must have really been stupid."

"That's all we can figure," Doug said. Then he motioned to Jonas' hand. "I really do hate to be pushy, but I would feel better if we removed the chip right now and destroyed it."

"Absolutely," Jonas said.

Doug had helped with a few other chip removals at the Hobble Creek Camp the previous fall, and had become quite skilled at it. If the chip had been in the person's hand for more than a few months it could be a little stubborn to remove, but a couple of precise cuts usually popped it right out.

Emma brought a well-stocked first aid kit to the table, and after numbing the back of Jonas's hand, Doug made a small incision and removed the chip. It came out more easily than they had expected, and the cut hardly bled. Doug actually used super glue rather than stitches to close up the incision and then wrapped it tightly.

"Whew, that went smoothly," Jonas said, truly relieved that it hadn't been too painful.

Emma briefly stepped out of the room and returned with a hammer. "There's just one more step to the process—smashing it," she said. "Would you like to do the honors?"

Doug put the chip on a small piece of gauze and placed it on the floor, then Jonas enthusiastically swung the hammer at it with his left hand, missing it by an inch. "Strike one," he said a little sheepishly. His second swing hit the mark, and Emma applauded.

"You're free," Doug said.

Later that evening Jonas was introduced to Emma's children, who were just coming home from an activity at the meetinghouse.

"Children, this is Jonas . . ." Emma said. "Um, sorry, Jonas, I guess I never got your last name."

"Fer . . . guson." he stammered. "Jonas Ferguson."

Emma smiled. "Anyway kids, Jonas knew Daddy when he was working at the City Creek Center."

Leah and Charles shook hands with him, then went outside to play in the fading sunlight. As they shut the door, the details of Tad's CCA file suddenly popped into Jonas' head. He turned to Emma. "I thought Tad said you had three kids."

"We do. David is with Tad as part of the Manti Men."

He slapped his forehead. "Oh, of course. Tad was so proud of him. Well, I wish them both the best. I'm glad they are willing to defend our country."

Emma smiled. "I really would have preferred for David to stay home with me, but there was no way I was going to convince him to stay. To be honest, he's probably in better shape to be a soldier than Tad is."

Jonas smiled. "I don't know about that. Tad was in pretty good shape. So with a good portion of the men gone with the army, how many men are still here?"

Emma thought for a moment. "Probably a thousand, but most of them are older, since they are high priests—like Doug here."

Doug laughed at the gentle teasing from his sister. "The women and children definitely outnumber the men at the moment, but everything is working out."

"Yes, everything seems to be running smoothly," Jonas said. "I was wondering about the outlying towns, though. Richard and I stayed in a small town last night, and there were quite a few families living there. Are there lots of little settlements like that? I guess I figured everyone would be living here near the temple."

"There are at least 10,000 people living in the valley, not counting the soldiers that are gone," Doug said. "You see, last fall more than twenty groups gathered here from the smaller mountain camps. Our group was one of the first to arrive, so we naturally settled close to the temple here in Manti. But as more groups came, there just wasn't enough room here in Manti, even if we doubled up the housing like we did, so they started assigning the groups to the surrounding towns."

"Wow, that's a lot of people," Jonas said. "Do you ever get together all at once?"

"Not too often. Of course, when the prophet came last fall, we all gathered at the temple."

Jonas' ears perked up. "You said the prophet was here?"

"Yes, we had a wonderful meeting."

"Where is he now?" Jonas couldn't even imagine what a prize the prophet would be for Sherem!

"He left soon afterward," Doug said. "I think he's on the move a lot to avoid being captured or killed. There are still a lot of people in these mountains who would love to harm him. You never know what Satan might inspire someone to do."

"I agree," Jonas said, feeling slightly guilty. "I would have liked to see him, though."

The families soon knelt together in the living room for a family prayer, and then Doug invited Jonas to sleep on the couch. "We'll look for better accommodations for you in the morning, but this will have to do for tonight."

"This is great," Jonas said. It was clear that Doug had no inkling that his houseguest only intended to stay until around midnight before sneaking out and returning to Nephi.

Doug and Emma had provided him with plenty of information. The group had some weapons, but for the most part they were defenseless. Plus, the groups were scattered enough throughout the valley that Sherem's army could easily go from town to town without much opposition. Jonas estimated that within a week the rampage would be over, and he would be hailed as a hero.

Chapter 14

Jonas lay on the couch in the darkness and pulled a blanket over himself as he listened as the household settle down. He actually drifted off to sleep for a few minutes before a baby's cry came from a bedroom. He hadn't even realized there was a baby in the house.

Jonas heard someone shuffling around, and then Doug emerged from the bedroom carrying a baby wrapped in a blanket. He sat in the darkness in a chair across the room, and the baby quieted down.

"Hey, Doug, who have you got there?" Jonas said softly.

"Oh, I'm sorry if I woke you," Doug whispered. "This is Daniel, our little boy. He's been asleep all evening. I usually get up with him if he cries during the night. I like to let Becky get all the sleep she can."

"That's very nice of you," Jonas said, once again feeling that annoying twinge of guilt for the part he would play in their approaching deaths.

"Hey, since you're awake could you hold Daniel for a minute?" Doug asked. "Becky had pumped some breastmilk into a bottle for him, and I need to get it out of the icebox and warmed up."

"Uh, sure," Jonas said. He hadn't held a baby in many years, but he knew he had to maintain his role as a good-hearted man at least until Doug went back to bed. Then he would be on his way back to Nephi.

"We call Daniel our miracle baby," Doug whispered. "He was born without an arm and has some other physical problems, but he has really fought to stay on this earth. Plus, he has brought a special feeling of love to our home." Doug handed Daniel to Jonas, then lit a small candle on a small table. "I'll be back in a minute."

Jonas was admittedly curious about Daniel's missing arm. He moved the baby's blanket slightly and saw that indeed the little boy was missing a limb. He couldn't help but feel a bit of compassion. "That's a rough way to start your life, little Daniel," he said.

But then Jonas was taken aback as he looked into the baby's eyes. Even though the light from the candle wasn't very bright, it was clear that Daniel was staring straight at him, and it wasn't the gaze of an infant. Jonas felt like he was looking into the eyes of an old, wise soul who seemed to be aware of his evil intentions.

Jonas looked toward the kitchen, hoping Doug would hurry so he could give Daniel back to him, but he wasn't anywhere to be seen.

"Hey, just close your eyes and go to sleep, little boy," Jonas whispered. But Daniel continued to stare intently at him.

Out of nowhere came his Bible teacher Sister Hall's voice, "*But whoso should offend one of these little ones which believe in me, it were better for him that a millstone were hanged about his neck, and that he were drowned in the depths of the sea.*"

Jonas looked around for whoever had spoken to him, but no one else was in sight. He looked down at Daniel, who seemed to now be smiling. "This is crazy," he whispered.

The baby then continued to stare at him as intently as before, but now with a pleading look in his eyes. Jonas felt goosebumps race up and down his entire body. He was close to freaking out.

Sister Hall's voice came again, "*Take heed that ye despise not one of these little ones.*"

"This is too much," Jonas whispered. He was nearly ready to leave the baby on the couch and take off out the door, but just then Doug entered the room again.

"Good job," Doug whispered. "It looks like you have the magic touch with babies."

Jonas shook his head. "What do you mean?" Then he looked down at Daniel. To his surprise the baby's eyes were closed and he appeared to be sleeping soundly. Doug came over to retrieve him, and as Jonas handed Daniel back to his father, the baby turned toward Jonas and gave him one final pleading look before Doug blew out the candle, causing Jonas to squirm once again.

Doug stepped toward the bedroom. "Now that I've got the bottle, I'll take Daniel back to our room so you can get to sleep. Thanks again."

"No problem," Jonas said, struggling to keep his voice steady. As Doug closed the bedroom door, Jonas' mind raced as he tried to comprehend what had just happened. That cursed baby seemed to know what he was thinking!

He felt a panic in his chest. He still intended to go through with Sherem's plan and felt justified in it, but deep down he began to worry that God would hold him accountable for the deaths of everyone who would soon be killed in the valley. On the other hand, he feared being killed by Sherem's men if he betrayed them. "What have I gotten myself into?" he whispered in despair.

Jonas felt paralyzed by his emotions, unable to leave the couch. How could he ever forgive himself if he caused the death of a precious one-armed newborn? The debate in his mind raged on throughout the night, and he eventually drifted off to sleep in the early morning hours, as troubled as ever. But when he awoke the next morning he finally came to one conclusion: "I can't kill these people!"

He climbed off the couch and knocked softly on Doug's bedroom door. When Doug cracked it open, Jonas said, "We really need to talk—right now."

Doug quickly pulled his clothes on, and they began walking outside in the brisk morning air. After a few moments, Jonas stopped and looked Doug in the eyes. "Someday you need to thank your son Daniel for saving everyone in this valley."

"How could that be? I don't understand."

Jonas hung his head, disgusted with himself. "I've been lying to you ever since I arrived here. If you hadn't given me Daniel to hold last night, I would have left your house at midnight to let a blood-thirsty army stationed in Nephi know that they could come here and slaughter you all."

Jonas then quickly explained about Sherem and his evil plans. Doug felt like he'd been punched in the stomach, partly because he realized how gullible he had been to fall for Jonas' lies.

"What do we do now?" Doug asked frantically. "Do you think we could defend ourselves against them?"

"Not a chance. These are hardened criminals who have already killed hundreds of people in Salt Lake. They each have at least one gun with plenty of ammunition. The only option now is to move everyone out of the valley. Sherem's army is waiting for me to return and tell them about the conditions here, but if I don't show up within a couple of days, I'll bet they'll come into the valley anyway."

Doug began running toward President Johnson's house. "Follow me. You need to explain this to our leaders."

They quickly arrived at the president's house, where Doug and Jonas filled him in on the situation. Everyone agreed that an evacuation was the only answer, and messengers were sent to spread the word through the stake and ward priesthood leaders that an attack was imminent.

Soon all of the leaders had been informed about the evacuation plan to have everyone leave out of the south end of the valley and regroup in the town of Salina several miles away.

Each ward was already organized with capable high priests serving as "block captains" who were in charge of several families, and every member of the ward knew their own responsibility. Jonas watched in amazement as the evacuation unfolded without a hitch. He asked Doug, "How does everyone know what to do?"

"We've known something like this could happen, so during the past few months we've held training sessions to get everyone prepared. Of course, we had expected the army to be Coalition soldiers, rather than escapees from the state prison."

Doug knew he needed to get back to his own house, but first he grabbed Jonas by the arm. "Hey, I want to thank you, but I also want to know if I can trust you. This isn't some sort of perverse trick, is it? Please tell me we aren't going to get to Salina and find Sherem's army waiting for us."

Jonas was a little surprised. "You have my word. For the first time in a long time, I feel like I've done the right thing."

Doug nodded. "I'm happy to hear that, but it might be best if we don't tell Becky or Emma your role in the evacuation. The time might come for you to explain all of this, but not right now."

"I agree," Jonas said, and they went their separate ways to continue the preparations. Jonas stayed busy helping Emma and Becky load their remaining food into handcarts.

Of course, Jonas was still harboring other secrets that the family certainly didn't want to know—such as that he was the very CCA officer who had sought to kill their beloved Tad. He wasn't sure he would ever have the courage to share that information with them, and he hoped that if he ever saw Tad again that he wouldn't recognize him. He decided at that moment to let his hair grow out so Tad wouldn't recognize him.

But Jonas was able to soon put those worries aside, because he was struggling with a feeling in his chest that he hadn't felt since his youth—a sense of happiness and warmth, replacing layers of bitterness and darkness.

The feeling literally brought him to his knees as he walked to the backyard to retrieve another handcart from the tent. He bowed his head and said, "Dear God, if my soul is worth saving, I hope this is the start."

Chapter 15

Richard Dalton had spent a pleasant evening in Manti with his wife and children. He was preparing to return to his assignment in Salt Creek Canyon that morning when the announcement came to evacuate the valley. He stayed to help his family get packed when he was summoned to meet with President Johnson at the stake center.

Richard found President Johnson outside the stake center loading supplies onto a wagon, but when the president spotted Richard, he hurried him right into his office and closed the door.

"I'm so glad you're in town," President Johnson said. "I'm sure you've heard the reports, but I need you to verify that there's an army in Nephi camped near the mouth of the canyon."

Richard was a little bewildered. "How did we hear about this? I've been at that guard post most of the winter and there hasn't been any sign that we are going to be attacked."

"I understand, and I don't have time to go into the details, but that's why I want you to check it out. Meanwhile, we'll continue the evacuation. If this is a false alarm, it will have been good training—but I sense this is the real thing. It confirms the strong promptings I've been feeling the past week that we would be leaving the valley soon."

"I'll take off immediately," Richard said. "What should I do if I see that there really is an army there?"

"Follow the plan we've set up for the canyon. It might buy us a little extra time. Then I need you to safeguard the temple. As you know, we'll travel to Salina. That should get us far enough away. But if the army detects our trail and starts following us, do everything you can to let us know. Once we reach Salina, I'll send some men back to check on things, but at the moment we need every man we have."

"I understand," Richard said. "I'll do my best."

Richard pushed his horse as much as he could throughout the day and reached his guard post in the canyon by late afternoon. He took a moment to eat a quick meal and explain the situation to his fellow guard, Chris, but within ten minutes he was riding toward Nephi on a fresh horse from the barn. Every muscle in his body ached, but if there was really an army of ex-convicts camped in Nephi waiting to attack the valley, he knew there wasn't time to worry about anything else.

It was already dark as he approached the mouth of Salt Creek Canyon, and he got off the paved road as quickly as he could to soften the clomping of the horse's hooves. He proceeded slowly in case the enemy had guards watching, but it appeared he hadn't been spotted. President Johnson had told him the army was camped in the Wendy's parking lot just west of the freeway.

Unfortunately, the freeway overpass blocked his view, so he prodded the horse to climb higher up the foothills, and soon several campfires could be seen next to the restaurant and he could see dozens of tents set up in rows in the parking lot and the road. Thankfully there was a full moon, and Richard could see there were hundreds of men gathered around the campfires, if not thousands. He strained to listen and could hear their boisterous laughter.

"This is not good," he said to himself. "I better take care of this tonight."

Richard rode back up the canyon about a mile to a spot where the canyon narrowed. The previous fall before the snow had come, he and several other men had planted several powerful explosives in both sides of the mountainside, then rigged them to be activated from one central detonation point.

The idea was to create a pair of rockslides that would block the canyon at this narrow point, as well as cause Salt Creek to be dammed off. The men had hoped such a blockade would stop—or at least delay—anyone trying to invade the canyon. Now it was time to test whether their hard work the past fall was worth it.

The detonation box had been carefully hidden about 500 yards from where the explosives had been planted. Richard found the box and unlatched the lid. He was happy to see the inside of the box was dry, and he grabbed a large battery from the corner of the box that was wrapped in plastic. He connected the battery to the terminal and said a quick prayer, then pressed the detonation switch. He could see the explosion area from the detonation box, and he was glad to see some puffs of smoke. Five seconds later the rumbling began, and then it grew into a crescendo of rocks being blown from the mountainside. He could even see large boulders plummeting to the canyon floor.

"Whew, it worked even better than we had hoped," Richard said with relief. He got back on his horse and moved forward to get a better view of his handiwork. The full moon illuminated large billows of dust climbing into the sky, and he could see a 40-foot-high wall of rocks where the road had been earlier. But he really wanted to see if the creek and been blocked, and he was thrilled to see the water already forming a large pool all the way across the canyon behind the newly formed dam.

"Well, that should hopefully slow them down," he told himself.

He stopped at the guard house to retrieve Chris, and they headed back toward Manti. Once they were out of the canyon, they found a grove of trees to catch a few hours of sleep, but they were back on their horses by sunrise.

As they passed through the towns of Fountain Green and Moroni, nearly all of the Saints that had been living there were already heading south. There were a few families who weren't finished packing yet, but as Richard rode past them, he informed them there was indeed an invading army in Nephi. He couldn't help but smile as the families suddenly picked up their pace.

Richard's partner Chris lived in Ephraim, and they checked his home, but his family had already departed. So they traveled to Manti, where Richard stopped at the Manti Temple and Chris planned to continue on to catch up with his family and report to President Johnson about the army.

"Tell Melanie I will catch up with her as soon as I can," Richard told him. "President Johnson just wants me to keep an eye on the temple for now—and to see if the army ends up following us."

By evening, Richard was the only Saint left in the valley. He hid his horse on the far side of the temple, then he carefully checked the barricades that had been constructed in front of the temple doorways. Finally, he fastened the final section of the 12-foot-high electric fence into place that had been installed as a protection around every temple the United States. It was a relief to flip on the switch that energized the fence and finally take a well-deserved rest. He made himself a bed on a couch in the temple's visitors center and drifted off to sleep.

Chapter 16

A few miles to the west, Ken Turner was pacing restlessly along the freeway overpass in Nephi as he kept an eye on the mouth of Salt Creek Canyon. It was now the third day since Jonas had headed to Manti, and Ken expected him to return at any time.

Ken's main worry was that Sherem's men were getting extremely restless. To amuse themselves, they were tearing apart the Wendy's restaurant piece by piece and then burning whatever they had ripped loose. The criminals really had a great time melting each of the plastic tables, but the highlight so far had been watching the soda dispenser twist and pop as it bubbled down into a big hunk of plastic and metal.

The night before, the men had heard loud rumblings coming from the canyon, and the creek the army was using as their water source had transformed from a flowing stream into a mere trickle by morning. It was clear something strange had happened.

Ken was coming to the conclusion that the Mormons hadn't believed Jonas' story and had probably tortured him mercilessly to get the truth out of him. If that was the case, Ken didn't have any time to lose. He climbed down from the overpass and gathered the leaders of Sherem's army together. "Jonas should have been back by now," Ken told them. "I'll bet they've captured him. We need to get there and finish them off before they can escape somewhere."

One of the men said, "I brought along one of those chip detectors that we used while raiding the Salt Lake neighborhoods. It would help us see where Jonas is."

Ken's eyes widened. "I didn't know we had one of those things.

Why didn't you tell me that before? Go get it! We'll use it to find Jonas when we get to Manti. We haven't got any time to lose if we're going to save him."

Ken climbed onto a smoldering pile of debris from the Wendy's building and called for everyone's attention. Once all of the men were listening, he shouted, "The Mormons have probably killed our friend Jonas, and the time has come for vengeance. We must act immediately. Grab your weapons and follow me to the canyon!"

Sherem's army gave a shout of deranged glee, and as Ken climbed down from the building, grabbed his rifle and sprinted toward the canyon, the rest of the men joined right in. In their hysteria, they left their tents and their remaining food, not expecting to need it once they found the Mormons. Sherem's men were hardened both physically and spiritually, and Ken estimated that they could easily be in Manti by the following morning if they pushed themselves.

But within a mile a huge obstacle rose up in front of them. Ken moved to the front of the group and stared at the pile of rubble that blocked the canyon. A few of the men were already scaling it, but it was extremely unstable, and they accidentally sent several small boulders tumbling down toward the army.

"Hey, get down!" Ken shouted. "You keep knocking rocks loose. You're going to kill one of us."

A couple of the men ignored him and within a few minutes made it to the top of the rubble. But as they looked over the edge, they were surprised to see a small lake had formed.

"I found our water problem," one of them called out. "The stream is backed up and formed a lake."

Ken was starting to get really irritated. "This must have been the rumbling we heard," he said. Then he pointed at the canyon walls. "Look at this. It came down both sides. That just isn't natural. I'll bet the Mormons did this. They must have known we were coming."

They only had one option—to climb up the steep hillside to get around the landslide and the lake. By the time all of the men had reached the road again on the far side of the lake, the sun had already gone down. They kept moving up the road in the darkness until the canyon widened a little.

"This will have to do for tonight," Ken said, disgusted at their slow progress. "Find a place to sleep, but we're marching again at the crack of dawn."

The next day Sherem's men made great time and made it all the way to the city of Moroni. Some of the men were bothered that the town was empty, but Ken assured them all of the Mormons were gathered around their temple in Manti. He declared, "By this time tomorrow you will have annihilated the Mormons and be feasting like kings!"

Richard Dalton woke up with a start as sunlight filtered into the temple visitors center. During the night he had experienced a vivid dream in which he watched a swarming army approach Manti on the highway from Ephraim.

The men seemed extremely frustrated, and there was a lot of bickering among them. The army soon congregated in front of the temple, and their leaders seemed to be reading a message that was written on a large piece of plywood that had been placed there.

In the dream, Richard watched the leaders have an animated discussion. Some of the leaders kept pointing south in the direction the Saints had actually gone, but one man kept pointing north from where they had just come. In the end, the army had departed back up the road to Ephraim.

After they were out of sight, Richard saw himself walk down in front of the temple to see what was on the wooden sign. It read:

Attention everyone!
An army is coming to kill us!
Evacuate to the town of Birdseye
in Spanish Fork Canyon!
<----- <-----

As Richard pondered the dream, he knew it was a message from the Lord. He pulled on his clothes and hurried to a maintenance shed where he found a large piece of plywood that looked exactly like the one he had seen in his dream. He dragged it down the hill and propped it lengthwise against a rock just inside the electric fence where the army would most likely approach first. Then he located a can of red paint and a paintbrush, and began writing that same message on the plywood.

The words looked rather crude, but he felt it looked better that way, hoping that if the army ever actually read it, they would feel it was written hastily for the Saints, rather than being a way to throw them off course.

He smiled as he added the two arrows he had seen in his dream that pointed north toward Spanish Fork Canyon. "These guys must need an extra dose of convincing if the Lord wants me to put arrows on the sign," he said to himself. "Oh well, better safe than sorry."

He put away the paint and brush, and then took a padded chair from the visitors center and carried it to the highest point on the temple property. He also had binoculars with him, and every few minutes he would check the road coming out of Ephraim. Any doubts he may have had about whether the army would come had been erased by the dream. He knew it was only a matter of time before those hordes of men would reach Manti.

As Ken led Sherem's men past the McDonald's restaurant on the southern outskirts of Ephraim, he knew they would soon be in sight of the temple. He had stopped at that McDonald's several times after temple trips to Manti in his younger days. He briefly pondered how life had changed so drastically, but at the moment he felt a sense of power that he had never experienced before. He realized if the army gained control of Manti, then Sherem would likely choose him as the ruler of this area. It was a great feeling.

The temple soon came into view, and Ken shouted, "There it is! Sherem might have his home in the State Capitol Building, but I'll make the Manti Temple my castle."

Ken didn't realize that some of Sherem's men took his comment both as a slam to Sherem and also as a very arrogant hint that Ken thought he ruled them. Many of the men were already tired of Ken's condescending tone with them, but for now they kept quiet. If there truly were Mormons in Manti, then the men would take their spoils and be happy. But if not . . .

Richard suddenly spotted the army quickly approaching over the nearest hill. Many of them were actually running down the road and would reach the temple soon. Richard hurried out of sight and moved to a hidden clump of shrubs within earshot of where he had placed the wooden sign. He knew it was risky, but he really wanted to hear what the leaders discussed.

Within ten minutes, the army was gathered in front of the temple, and one man stood facing them, clearly the leader. Somebody called out, "Ken, where are all of the Mormons?"

"It looks like they must have heard we were coming. But don't worry, we'll catch up with them. Look. They were foolish enough to leave out a sign they had made."

Ken turned around and pointed at the sign Richard had made earlier in the day. "I know where Birdseye is, and it would make a perfect hiding place for a large group of people. It's tucked away in the mountains, and they could live there safely for months. No one would even know they were there. But they'll be surprised when we show up!"

Another man stepped forward. "The arrows on the sign point back in the direction we just came. Why would they go that way? I'll bet this is a trick. I think they're headed south and are trying to outrun us."

Ken smiled. "So you're saying this sign isn't real? It's clear that they knew we were on our way, but do you really believe in the midst of their panic that somebody took the time to make a fake sign? Look at it. That message was obviously written by someone in a big hurry. I'm as disappointed as you are that the Mormons somehow slipped past us, but we'll find them."

Just then one of the men leaned against the fence and got a nice jolt of electricity. He squirmed on the ground for a moment, then let out a loud cry of pain as everyone stepped back a couple of paces. Then he sat up and seemed to recover.

"He'll be fine," Ken said. "The same thing happened to me in Salt Lake."

Once Ken got the army's attention again, he said, "Look, I understand your logic, but it isn't that hard to figure out. Somebody scrawled the sign to warn anyone who might have fallen behind the group, then he turned on the electricity and took off."

"Then how come we didn't see anybody on our way here?" another man asked.

"We probably just missed them as we came into Ephraim," Ken said. "Trust me! I would bet on my own life that we'll find the Mormons hiding in the town of Birdseye. We can be there by tomorrow if we leave right now."

Ken then started marching north again, and although it took a few minutes for some of the reluctant ones to follow, soon all of the men were heading back toward Ephraim.

Richard offered a prayer of thanks and wearily made his way back to the visitors center.

Three days later, Richard hadn't seen any additional sign of the army, yet he didn't feel confident about leaving the temple. Then to his surprise he saw his fellow guard Chris ride up on his horse. Richard quickly turned off the power to the electric fence and let him inside.

"How's everything going with the Saints?" Richard asked as he closed the gate and got the power turned back on.

"Very well," Chris said. The group made it to Gunnison last

night and left this morning for Salina. President Johnson sent me back to check on you. Have you seen the army yet?"

"Oh, they've been here, and we would have been in big trouble if we hadn't left when we did," Richard said. "They nearly headed south and probably would have easily caught up to our group by now, but I received a little inspiration and sent them a different way."

He turned and pointed to his wooden sign. Chris read it and started laughing. "They fell for that?"

Richard smiled. "I guess it proves that through small things great things come to pass."

"So they headed to Birdseye?"

"I lost sight of them once they got near Ephraim, but I really want to check on what happened to them before we leave Manti. If you can stay here, I'll ride out to Birdseye and see what I find. If everything looks all right, we'll catch up with our families."

"Sounds good," Chris said. "I think I'll stay safely behind the electrical fence until you get back, though."

Two days later, Richard rode into the outskirts of Birdseye. As he approached the little white church where he had once attended meetings with his family, there was evidence of a brutal battle. There were dozens of bodies scattered around the parking lot. He recognized them as being from the group that had argued with each other in front of the temple.

Most of the men had been shot, but a few had been stabbed. Richard was horrified by the sight. In his mind's eye he could picture the group reaching Birdseye and not finding any Mormons. It was likely the final straw for some of the men—combined with exhaustion and a lack of food—leading to bloodshed as the wicked killed the wicked.

Richard could see some evidences, such as footprints in the mud and a few blood trails, that the battle's survivors must have headed north on the highway. He realized they were probably headed down Spanish Fork Canyon and into Utah County. He didn't care where they went, as long as they were heading away from the Saints.

As Richard was about to return to Manti, he spotted a body hanging from a small tree near the meetinghouse. Everyone else had been left to die where they had fallen, but this person had clearly been singled out by the survivors of the battle.

Richard moved closer, and he noticed that hooked over a button on the man's shirt was a note written on Church stationery taken from the meetinghouse. It read: "*Here hangs the all-knowing Ken Turner. He bet his life on finding the Mormons here. He was wrong.*"

Chapter 17

As the evacuation of Manti was taking place, the members of the Manti Men were unaware of what was happening to their family members. They were enduring a grueling march of their own. They had turned onto I-84 at Ogden, and were now making their way through snow-filled mountain passes on their way to Wyoming. They merged with I-80 and the snow continued to get deeper the further north they traveled.

Long stretches of the freeway were coated with ice, and climbing some of those frozen inclines was a treacherous process. Many times men would nearly reach the top of a hill before losing their footing and tumbling all the way to the bottom, usually taking out a few other men with them. The resulting injuries slowed the group even more as the wounds were treated. Tad and David were grateful they had somehow avoided those nasty spills.

With great happiness they reached the town of Evanston, Wyoming on a Sunday and were able to spend a portion of the day indoors at a pair of LDS meetinghouses. It was crowded inside the buildings, but it was such a relief to get out of the cold.

After the difficult hike through the mountains, the remaining march to Fort Bridger the next three days seemed like a walk in the park. The Manti Men arrived at the fort just as other groups were also arriving there from throughout the Rocky Mountains.

Tad looked around at the multiplying numbers and finally felt that they were assembling an army that could hold their own against the Coalition soldiers.

The next two days were filled with organizing themselves into units of 1,000 soldiers, with captains over groups of 100. The Manti Men stayed together for the most part, while some of the smaller groups were combined to fill out the ranks. There were elders of every race from all over the western United States and Canada. They had each heeded the prophet's call the previous year to go to the mountain camps, and now they were part of the Lord's army—faithful members of the Elders of Israel.

There were a total of 8,000 soldiers—an imposing number, but a total likely dwarfed by the Coalition's forces. They trained together, and while many of the men had brought a rifle with them, many had not, and there was quick but thorough marksmanship training and target practice. David secretly prayed that he would never have to take the life of an enemy solider, but he was willing to do so if it became necessary.

Sunday arrived once again, and the thousands of soldiers gathered in an open field outside Fort Bridger's main buildings after eating lunch.

A large screen had been put in place against one of the buildings, and soon a scene of an empty pulpit was shown. Then the prophet was wheeled up to it by one of the apostles.

"My dear brethren, I hope you had a good lunch on this beautiful Sabbath day. I am speaking to you from the lobby of the Rexburg Temple, and as you can see, my legs have decided to act their age again. So please forgive me for giving this message sitting down, but it is better than giving it flat on my back."

The men laughed, and the prophet continued, "Many of you might not be aware that on the site where you are standing, valiant elders of the Church fought against the advance of Johnston's Army in the 1850s. The elders even burned the original buildings to the ground in an effort to stop that army. They truly gave their best effort to help protect the Church.

"Now we face an even greater enemy in the Coalition forces that are gathered at Kansas City. Several of our courageous elders have been monitoring the Coalition's movements and conversations, and every indication is that they will start moving west across Kansas within two weeks. It is absolutely essential that we have your army in Denver by that time. Otherwise the Coalition will divide its forces at that point and begin to spread throughout the West. They plan to sweep through the Rocky Mountains and then claim the entire land as theirs."

The prophet then raised his hand in a fist. "They have miscalculated, however. They seem unaware of the large numbers of Latter-day Saints living in these mountains, and that an army has been raised up—according to prophecy—that will defend the land and preserve our liberty. My dear brethren, you will fulfill that prophecy!"

A roar went up from among the elders. Tad looked over at David, and they smiled at each other. The prophet added, "The errand you are going to undertake will be difficult, but you will have angels attending you, and I know the Lord is at your side. Your leaders report that your training has gone well, and we have instructed them to begin the march to Denver tomorrow."

The men clapped and a few whistled. Everyone was ready to move forward. The prophet closed his message by saying, "Ye Elders of Israel, we salute you. The First Presidency and the apostles that are here wish to bid you farewell with a simple hymn of brotherhood. We'll only sing one verse, and it won't be pitch-perfect, but please know it is certainly heartfelt."

The camera panned backward, and several of the apostles were shown. They grouped together and sang:

Behold, a royal army, with banner, sword, and shield,
is marching forth to conquer on life's great battlefield.
Its ranks are filled with soldiers, united, bold and strong,
who follow their Commander and sing their joyful song:
Victory, victory, through him that redeemed us!
Victory, victory, through Jesus Christ our Lord!
Victory, victory, victory, through Jesus Christ our Lord!

The group of elders felt an surge of the Spirit pass through them, testifying that the words the Lord's apostles were singing were true, and many wept openly.

Following the song, the prophet said, "You may have noticed that Elder Smith is not with us. He's making his way to you right now from Salt Lake, and expects to join you by morning. As the presiding priesthood leader, he's authorized to make key decisions and to seek the will of the Lord in regard to military planning. Our thoughts and prayers are with you. Spend the rest of this holy day in prayer and supplication before the Lord. We all understand that many of you might not live through the battle that looms ahead. But I plead with you to purge from your heart any remaining wickedness and seek the guidance of the Holy Ghost. Then if it's your time to pass to the other side, your Savior can welcome you with open arms."

The following morning Elder Smith arrived in a horse-drawn sleigh, and soon afterward, the various units of the Elders of Israel began their march east along I-80. The snow had melted off the blacktop, and they made good time in reaching Cheyenne, where they regrouped for a day before heading south on I-25. It was a welcome sight to see the skyscrapers of downtown Denver rise up ahead of them.

The previous fall, the Coalition leaders had sent a fleet of tanks along I-70 to destroy military bases in Colorado Springs and near Denver. The bases had been destroyed, and then the tanks had moved eastward on their mission, ignoring Denver itself.

The city's citizens had been grateful to be spared from a Coalition attack, but it soon became clear that the winter months were going to be unbearable. Food was already scarce, and most of the population soon departed for warmer parts of the country. By January, the snow in Denver had piled up above the housetops. So now as the snow rapidly melted away, the city looked pristine but lacked any inhabitants.

Under the direction of Elder Smith, as the elders approached Denver they skirted around the empty city and settled into the abandoned homes in Aurora, a suburb on Denver's east side. The elders set up camps on both sides of I-70, expecting to begin the defense of their land right there on the frozen plains that stretched out before them.

Now all they could do was wait for the enemy to arrive.

Chapter 18

Before the United States dissolved, the small town of Salina in central Utah was best known to travelers as the last stop heading east along I-70 before hitting a long, barren stretch to the town of Green River. Now it was the home to the thousands of Saints that had fled Manti.

The members set up similar housing situations, with two or more families sharing a home. There still wasn't electricity, but there was plenty of water in the nearby creek. Everyone was on edge, wondering whether the invading army had somehow been stopped.

After discovering the massacre at Birdseye, Richard Dalton had returned to the Manti Temple, and his fellow guard Chris had agreed to stay and watch over the temple until instructed otherwise. Then Richard traveled all night to reach Salina. He knew the Saints wanted to know the outcome of the army's arrival.

He also wanted to see Jonas' reaction to the news. During his long ride, he had figured out that Jonas must have been the one who alerted the Saints about the army. But if so, Jonas had openly lied to him when they first met near the guard post. He had to know for himself that Jonas could be trusted and didn't have additional falsehoods up his sleeve.

Richard reached Salina's Main Street in mid-morning, and he immediately sought out President Johnson. The president spotted Richard's horse and waved him down.

"What's the report?" the president asked.

"I have great news," Richard responded. "The army did come

to Manti, but when they couldn't find any Mormons, they headed toward Spanish Fork Canyon instead. I followed behind them, and they ended up fighting each other at Birdseye. Their survivors appeared to have continued down the canyon to Utah County, rather than turn back. So Manti is safe."

Several members were listening in, and they gave shouts of relief. President Johnson motioned to them. "Spread the news! We are safe here."

"Where's Jonas?" Richard asked.

"Don't you want to see your family? Melanie and the kids are staying over on 100 East."

"I certainly do, but I really need to share something with Jonas first."

"He's staying with Doug Dalton," President Johnson said. "They're living in a house at the end of Main Street."

Richard followed the president's directions, and soon he saw Jonas sitting on the porch holding Doug's son Daniel. Richard waved as he approached, and Jonas said, "It's a relief that you made it safely. Did you see the army?"

"I did. Thankfully I tricked them into heading north instead of south, so we are safe here. But I have a question for you. Would you prefer Ken Turner dead or alive?"

Jonas jumped a little at the name. "I hope he's dead."

"Your wish has been granted," Richard said. Then he described the unsettling scene he had come across at Birdseye.

Jonas looked Richard in the eye. "As you have probably figured out, I lied to you in the canyon, and I'm sorry about that. But I had a change of heart once I met this little guy." He looked down at Daniel. "You can trust me. I never fit in with Sherem's army. I'm just grateful that I was the one sent to the valley. Any of those other guys were too hardened. They would've destroyed Manti."

Richard was satisfied with Jonas' response. He stuck out his hand. "Thank you, and welcome."

✣ ✣ ✣

Meanwhile, Emma North's nerves were starting to frazzle a little bit. She sat on her bed and wondered how much more she could take. It had been a year now since she and her family had really been together in their own home. When Tad had received the chip, she had moved with her kids to her parents' home in Springville, and then soon after came the call to gather to the Jolley's Ranch Camp in Hobble Creek Canyon.

This was followed by the prompting to go find her husband in Utah County, and then came their miraculous reunion with their group in Spanish Fork Canyon as they somehow avoided the Coalition tanks.

Then came the harsh winter in Manti. She was glad that if she had to share a house, at least it was with Doug and Becky. She greatly admired Becky, who had been a real strength to her, when it probably should have been the other way around.

After all, Becky had suffered a rough pregnancy compounded by the toxic cloud, and then to have Daniel arrive with physical ailments had been a shock to them all. Emma could tell that her sister-in-law still wasn't fully recovered from giving birth, yet Becky had kept a smile on her face through her challenges and even managed to take care of her two youngsters, Justin and Heather, without relying on others.

"I need to let her know how much I appreciate and admire her," Emma told herself.

Emma still couldn't quite shake out of her doldrums, though. She thought about the surprise call of Tad and David to serve with the Elders of Israel and how it had left her feeling empty inside. And now had come this unexpected move to Salina. President Johnson had said this was another step toward moving to New Jerusalem someday, but right now it just seemed like a big mess. Was this really part of a divine plan?

Emma had always envisioned the Saints making a triumphant, unimpeded march to Missouri with angels singing their praises along the way. That certainly didn't seem likely now. Everyone knew the clash between the Coalition forces and the Elders of Israel was imminent, and it sounded like the elders were outnumbered. Would she even see her husband and son again in this life?

"Heavenly Father, I will continue on the path thou hast provided for my family," Emma prayed. "Please give me the reassurance I need to move forward."

A few seconds later, she was surprised to hear these words in her mind. "*Have patience, my daughter. You aren't the only one facing challenges. Stay strong.*"

Emma's thoughts turned to her friend Kim Brown, and she knew that Josh and Kim had endured much more than she had. In a strange way, the thought of Kim's faithful perseverance lifted her spirits, and she hopped up to see if Charles and Leah were ready for lunch.

"Thank thee, Heavenly Father," Emma prayed as she left the room. "I know I'm very blessed. Please forgive me for whining once in a while."

Chapter 19

Kim Brown had felt stirrings in her stomach the past two days, and she sensed she was carrying a child. She thought back to her brief departure into the Spirit World a few months earlier when she had slipped and hit her head in the temple in Guatemala. Her memory was fading a little of what she experienced on the other side of the veil, but she remembered being shown two beautiful spirits, a boy and a girl, who were meant to be her children.

Along with the memory came the feeling that the children would not be born until she reached New Jerusalem, and she had looked forward with anticipation—she admittedly pictured herself giving birth in a gleaming hospital in the City of Zion. Of course, she had always figured that would include being pregnant in New Jerusalem, too, rather than in the middle of a desert.

She and Josh had been trying to have children since their first year of marriage, but the years had slipped away without them having a child. Then when they were called to serve in Guatemala, she reasoned that was part of the reason children hadn't come to them yet. But *now*?

She knew it was a bit selfish, but she prayed, "Dear Father, I know I'm carrying a child, but please somehow make it possible that I can give birth in thy holy city."

Kim actually did love living on the Hopi reservation, despite the limited electricity. It was comforting to be safely tucked away from the troubles happening all over the world. Plus, Kim had learned so much from both the Guatemalan and Hopi women, particularly on focusing on the important things in life. Most of these women had never even seen a DVD player or had a state-of-the art dishwasher, but they were constantly smiling, laughing, and helping each other. So after another morning of barely having enough energy to get out of bed, Kim finally stopped by the tent of her close friend Sister Mendoza, a Guatemalan sister with eight children. There had been several births among the group during the journey, and she had helped with many of them.

Kim found Sister Mendoza hanging a batch of newly washed clothing on a clothesline behind the tent. Her friend gave her a hug, and Kim whispered in her ear, "I have an important question for you. I think I'm pregnant. Can you help me know for certain?"

Sister Mendoza smiled. "I've been waiting for you to come talk with me. I had my suspicions. You need to talk to the Hopi doctor. I'll go with you this afternoon."

Kim was a little apprehensive—and slightly perturbed that her friend had apparently noticed her symptoms—but she agreed to go to the doctor. That afternoon Kim met with Brother Walking Eagle, a member of the Church who also had a small doctor's office in Polacca not too far from the meetinghouse.

Within minutes he determined that Kim was indeed pregnant and that she was actually nearly five months along.

"What? How did this happen?" Kim cried out. "We were in the middle of Mexico five months ago . . . oh, I remember now." Then she joined Brother Walking Eagle and Sister Mendoza in a good laugh. Sister Mendoza gave her a big hug. "You're so good with my children—and all of the children—that I know you're going to be a wonderful mother."

"Thank you! I want to tell Josh. He'll be so excited! He's been waiting for this day as anxiously as I have." Kim looked at the clock on Brother Walking Eagle's wall. "He should be back from meeting with the tribal leaders within an hour."

The doctor nodded. "Then let's finish up with the examination and make sure everything is okay, and then you can go tell everyone the good news!"

At that moment Josh and Mathoni were indeed finishing up a very inspiring meeting with the Hopi leaders. Several of the Guatemalan stake presidents were also in attendance. There had been a great feeling of brotherhood and unity throughout the meeting. The leaders had decided to invite all LDS Hopi families to join the Guatemalan Saints when they departed for Missouri after the war was over. This would be a voluntary decision, and no one would be forced to leave. As one Hopi leader pointed out, there were many non-LDS Hopi families who were perfectly content to stay in Hopiland.

As the decision was made, Josh looked around the room and felt almost overwhelmed to be in attendance at such a historic meeting. Both the Hopis and the Guatemalans had long-standing traditions that the time would come when they would help prepare the way for the return of the Great White Brother. Some Hopi prophecies spoke of building a holy city to the east in preparation for his return. Now they were witnessing these events unfold.

Josh and Mathoni had discussed several times that although the oral prophecies had been distorted a little over the centuries, they were amazingly accurate. Mathoni had confirmed to him that both groups were descendants of people the Savior had visited following his resurrection, and their role in building Zion was a fulfillment of many prayers by righteous prophets.

As the meeting was coming to a close, Josh said, "To help us all better understand what lies ahead for this people, I would like to read a few verses from the Book of Mormon. Would that be all right?" He looked toward the non-LDS chief, who nodded his approval.

Josh told the group, "The Book of Mormon mentions how Jesus Christ—the Great White Brother—visited the people of this land. He spoke of a time when their descendants would work together to build New Jerusalem. We are witnessing the fulfillment of this scripture this day."

Josh then read verses from Third Nephi 21:22-25:

"But if they will repent and hearken unto my words, and harden not their hearts, I will establish my church among them, and they shall come in unto the covenant and be numbered among this the remnant of Jacob, unto whom I have given this land for their inheritance;

"And they shall assist my people, the remnant of Jacob, and also as many of the house of Israel as shall come, that they may build a city, which shall be called the New Jerusalem.

"And then shall they assist my people that they may be gathered in, who are scattered upon all the face of the land, in unto the New Jerusalem.

"And then shall the power of heaven come down among them; and I also will be in the midst."

Josh closed his scriptures and said, "These words were spoken by the Savior almost 2,000 years ago, and we have the privilege of seeing it be fulfilled. I hope you can feel the power of those words. If we do our part and build this city, blessings will be poured out upon us, and the Savior himself will walk among us. Is there any greater blessing that could happen to us?"

Josh felt that each of the leaders had grasped the magnitude of their assignment, and he could sense visitors in the room from the Spirit World—the valiant ancestors of these men—sharing their approval. It sent a tingle down his spine to comprehend what awaited them.

Mathoni put his hand on Josh's shoulder as they returned to the Guatemalan camp after the meeting. "You did a very good job in helping them understand their important role," he said. "My brethren hoped and prayed for this day to come to pass. I know they are celebrating in the Spirit World right now."

Josh turned to look at his Nephite friend. "I knew it! You saw them in the room, didn't you?"

Mathoni nodded. "Some of the greatest prophets who ever walked this land were there tonight. The Savior permitted them to listen in on our meeting because they are doing all they can to inspire and assist this people."

"That really is amazing, but I guess it makes sense that a prophet's work is never done."

"That's for sure. I remember the time during the Dark Ages when we were working so hard to get the Renaissance started in Europe. That one definitely took some assistance from the other side."

"So you got to leave the American continent?" Josh asked. "I guess I figured you were trapped here for some reason."

"Not at all," Mathoni said. "One of the first places I went after being translated was to Jerusalem. It meant a lot to me to be able to actually walk where the Savior had lived in mortality and then sacrificed his life for us. Then over the next few centuries I traveled to nearly every part of the earth—always doing my part to spread the gospel message, of course. But there were some key events that we all took part in to get the Enlightenment started."

Mathoni then spent the next few minutes telling Josh the behind-the scenes story of how Johannes Gutenberg received the inspiration for the printing press.

"That one got the ball rolling," Mathoni said. "We needed the press to be invented in order to start printing the Bible, which would get people ready for the restoration of the gospel. So I had a lot of fun with that one—except for the 15th century clothes. I felt ridiculous sometimes."

Josh laughed. "I guess that's the price you pay for living for 2,000 years. Nothing you wear ever stays in style."

"That's why I'll always be grateful for Levi Strauss," Mathoni said with a grin. "His jeans have made the past 150 years a lot easier for me when it comes to fashion."

As they approached the Guatemalan camp, they looked down the road, and there were two women standing near the Polacca meetinghouse. One seemed to be jumping up and down.

"Is that Kim?" Josh asked.

The women started running toward them, and soon Kim launched herself into Josh's arms, almost knocking him over.

"Whoa, I missed you too," Josh told her after she planted a big kiss on his lips. "But I've only been gone a few hours. What's the big occasion?"

"You're going to be a dad!" Kim said happily. "I'm pregnant—with twins!"

Josh felt like the breath had been knocked out of him, but he broke into a huge smile. "Really? That's fantastic!"

"Yep. As the doctor was finishing the exam, he found a second baby. I was surprised, but remember what I saw in the Spirit World when I fell last year?"

"I certainly do. There were two spirits there that would be our children."

Kim smiled. "It looks like they'll be coming together."

Chapter 20

Mitko Petrov was standing on a grassy slope looking down at the massive numbers of Coalition forces that had gathered at Kansas City, Missouri. The next day they would begin their march across Kansas toward the Rocky Mountains, where they expected to meet little resistance in their final sweep of the United States.

However, there was a genuine feeling among the soldiers of abandonment by their own countries. It had become clear that their mother nations, Russia and China, would not be sending any reinforcements.

The two countries were now embroiled in a battle that started as a minor border dispute that had quickly escalated into a serious war. Other countries in Asia were being forced to takes sides, and there was some fear that nuclear weapons might be used. At the very least, the war was occupying their forces there and distracting their leaders from what was happening in America.

During the early stages of the invasion, the Coalition forces had received information from spy satellites that had been essential in targeting groups of Americans. But they hadn't received any status updates for several weeks, and as they began their final preparations for the march westward, such data would have been invaluable.

As one Coalition soldier had put it, "They want us to conquer America, but they forgot about us. Why should I get killed for them?"

This change in attitude seemed to weaken the soldiers' resolve. They had come to America with promises of nice homes and a comfortable life for their families after the Coalition had finished off the Americans, but now most of them just wanted to get it over with. They realized there was little chance they would get to bring their families, and most of them just wanted to return home as soon as possible.

Mitko also noticed that the group of soldiers who had arrived from Arizona looked tanned and well-fed—almost too well-fed. They had experienced a lot of success while fishing in Lake Powell, as well as gorging on the food they had found abandoned in Flagstaff and Page. They now looked like out-of-shape fraternity boys rather than trained soldiers.

These developments gave Mitko hope. He knew with all of his heart that the Saints were still living in the mountains. Six months ago, before the horrible winter, the soldiers would have easily destroyed any resistance the Saints had put up. But now the playing field seemed to be evening out.

Another thing working in the Saints' favor was the Coalition leaders' lack of knowledge about what lay between Kansas City and Denver. They had maps of Kansas and Colorado, and they planned to move along I-70 from town to town each day. It had worked well for them throughout the eastern United States, where there had been a freeway exit and a shopping center every couple of miles. The leaders realized there probably wouldn't be a lot of food, but at least there would be shelter along the way.

Mitko watched and listened attentively to their plans, but he kept his mouth shut. Having served as a missionary throughout the area, he knew the real story. The towns that were shown on the map along I-70 were hardly the urban cities that the Coalition was expecting. In fact, some of those so-called towns were little more than a gas station and a few farmhouses.

In reality, the Coalition would face endless plains almost all the way to Denver. If the weather was rough, they might find themselves stranded in the middle of nowhere. Such a situation would surely beat them down, especially when it was combined with the lingering flu-like sickness that had bothered them all winter and was making its way through the camp once again.

As Mitko joined the Coalition forces as they marched out of Kansas City the next morning, he felt mixed emotions. He knew that New Jerusalem would someday be built in that very spot, and part of him wanted to just hide there until the Saints came again. He was on the verge of tears. Jumbled thoughts filled his head, and he wondered if Heavenly Father had forgotten about him. "Why was I put in this strange situation? I feel I am on the wrong side of this war. Why couldn't I have been born in America?"

Then came a calm assurance from the Spirit, testifying to him that he needed to stay with the Coalition on their march toward Denver. He breathed deeply and whispered, "I will do whatever you need, my dear Father."

Mitko looked back toward Missouri as the army crossed a bridge into Kansas, but he somehow sensed it wouldn't be the last time he would visit this place. As he walked along the freeway, he felt very antsy and tense. He had once watched the Kentucky Derby at a member's home during his mission, and he had marveled at how nervous some of the horses acted as they had approached the starting gate. He now understood how those horses felt. He sensed he would soon be off and running on whatever errand the Lord had waiting for him—and he could hardly wait for the race to start.

Chapter 21

The leaders of the Elders of Israel were huddled around a table studying a map of I-70 through Kansas. Courageous LDS spies had confirmed the Coalition forces had left Kansas City the previous morning and were marching west on I-70. Unfortunately, the spies had attempted to follow the army and were spotted. Their final radio transmission had been cries for help, followed by the sound of gunfire.

As the Church leaders listened in, it hadn't been clear whether the Coalition forces had obtained the spies' radio, but at this point it wasn't worth the risk of using the radios and potentially revealing their position.

So a new plan was needed that would allow the Saints to know the location of the Coalition forces. Elder Smith felt the best option was to send pairs of elders ahead to each of the communities along I-70. Then as the enemy was spotted on its advancement west, that pair of elders would travel to the previous community and give a report. Their message would then be relayed back through each of the communities, almost Pony Express style, until it reached the Church leaders outside of Denver.

A meeting was hastily called, and Elder Smith explained the new plan. "This will hopefully help us be able to monitor their movements without risking too many lives," Elder Smith said. "Of course, we need some men to take this challenge. You'll be literally in the face of the enemy, but your service will be invaluable."

Tad looked around the group. No one moved a muscle, or even looked up to catch Elder Smith's eye. It was no secret that the men were very worn out from their hurried march from Fort Bridger, and blisters and sore hamstrings were common. The thought of heading out across the plains without the safety of the full army wasn't very appealing to anyone.

Tad's foot that he had injured last year on West Mountain had started throbbing the day before, and he had mentally excused himself from the assignment when he suddenly felt an elbow in his ribs.

"Dad, we can do it," David whispered. Before Tad could even respond, David had his hand in the air. "Elder Smith, my dad and I will volunteer."

The apostle smiled at them. "Wonderful! That's one pair. We need at least six more pairs."

It took another minute or so, but soon seven pairs had agreed to serve as the lookout team. The rest of the army were dismissed, and the pairs met back around the maps on the table. Tad wasn't thrilled with what lay ahead, and he knew Emma would have been furious with him for allowing their son to be put in such a dangerous position. But he couldn't help but smile as he watched David standing next to Elder Smith and carefully studying the map of I-70.

David motioned for Tad to join him. "Look, there's a town a few miles into Kansas called Colby. Elder Smith thinks that should be the farthest lookout spot. Let's take it."

Tad gave a quick wink to Elder Smith, who was also enjoying David's enthusiasm, despite the serious circumstances. "That sounds good to me," Tad said. "Does that sound all right to you, Elder Smith?"

"Absolutely," the apostle said.

"Then let's get started."

Tad and David were each assigned a horse, and their saddlebags were stocked with a week's worth of food, along with a two-man tent and sleeping bags. After two days, they still hadn't reached the Colorado state line. That afternoon they watched a monstrous black cloud rise out of the west and spread across the sky. Soon a blizzard of epic proportions had surrounded them. They were in an area that had previously been a vast wheat field, so there wasn't anywhere to take shelter, but they spotted a small grove of trees along the road and hurried there to take cover.

They set up their tent and miraculously got a fire going as the snow began to pile up. Soon there were four inches of fresh snow, with no sign of the storm stopping.

"This isn't a typical storm, even compared to the bad ones we had this past winter," Tad told David. "This should stop the Coalition in its tracks."

As nightfall came, they stacked a large pile of branches and logs onto their fire and hoped it would burn throughout the night. They checked on the horses and sheltered them as much as they could, then shook the snow off the tent, climbed inside and zipped it shut. They each said a fervent prayer, then they burrowed into their sleeping bags for the night.

Chapter 22

The Coalition forces had been moving slowly across Kansas for a week, and as Mitko had expected, their leaders hadn't anticipated how sparse the land was. The army was encountering endless stretches of frozen, barren fields as they traveled toward Denver.

Their progress that particular day had been slowed by a monstrous snowstorm that struck so suddenly in the late afternoon that they couldn't even get their large 20-man tents set up. Most of the soldiers ended up sleeping huddled together on the ground as a foot of snow covered them throughout the night.

They were running low on food much sooner than expected because they hadn't found any cities to loot along the way. But at last they reached a sign that said "Welcome to Colorado" and they celebrated leaving the nightmare of Kansas behind them. Their leaders assured them that Denver wasn't much farther, and that plenty of food and shelter awaited them.

The soldiers that were suffering the worst were the ones who had "softened up" by spending a few weeks basking in the sun at Page, Arizona. They were now the ones falling like flies. Their lengthy walk to Kansas City less than a month earlier had definitely worn them out, and they probably should have recuperated longer before heading directly into the winter conditions. More than half of the Arizona soldiers had asked to be left along the highway, claiming they would catch up. But the latest blizzard had likely sealed their fate.

Also, a lot of the Coalition soldiers had arrived in Kansas City with the flu-like illness that had devastated the nation, and it had continued to spread among the soldiers. As they walked toward Denver, some simply collapsed in the snow along the road and were left behind. Of the 15,000 soldiers that had left Kansas City, only 7,000 had made it to Colorado.

Mitko wasn't suffering from the illness like his fellow soldiers, but he was so tired that sleeping on the frozen ground among his fellow soldiers didn't really bother him. His biggest obstacle was still the thought of having to battle his fellow Saints that were somewhere in the mountains.

As the snow continued to come down forcefully during the night, Mitko slipped away from the camp and crouched behind a small shrub several hundred yards from the group. He poured out his heart in prayer, but it seemed as if the heavens were closed.

Then his patriarchal blessing came to mind, which he had received from a Bulgarian patriarch just before leaving for his mission. It had been a great support for him, and before joining the Coalition army, he had memorized it, knowing he wouldn't be able to take a written copy with him. The blessing had been filled with references to a temple marriage, raising righteous children, and service in leadership positions in the Church.

Mitko shook his head, unable to see how any of these things could now be possible. Then he remembered one specific paragraph from the blessing that he had never understood. It had always confused him. It said, "*The power of God will be manifest through you like a winter storm stretching across the land. At the proper time, the Spirit will prompt you to accomplish what you have been called to do. Do not hesitate. Your actions will have a profound effect upon your fellow Saints.*"

Mitko looked at the snow piling up around him, and the Spirit hit him so forcefully that he felt the air go out of his lungs. A voice in his head said, "The time has come. Join your priesthood brethren."

Mitko was stunned, but he picked up his gun and quietly

moved toward I-70, cautiously looking back at the sleeping soldiers to the edge of the Coalition camp. No one stirred as he walked away, and the falling snow would quickly erase his tracks. Besides, after the number of deaths within their ranks the past few days, the leaders wouldn't even notice he had disappeared.

Mitko walked for several hours through the snow. He felt a mix of relief to be free from the Coalition, but also a sense of fear that the Saints wouldn't believe his story. By 3 a.m., the snow began to ease up. He was exhausted, and when he saw an abandoned car along the road, he decided to get some rest in the back seat.

As Mitko slept, his mind was filled with a strange scene. He found himself watching a large group of young men. He somehow knew this group was Helaman's 2,000 stripling warriors whose story was told in the Book of Mormon. The leaders of these young men were planning a strategy on how to outsmart the Lamanites. Mitko watched their plan smoothly unfold, resulting in a stunning Nephite victory.

He awoke with a start as a voice said, "That is the plan you must share with your priesthood brethren. Go now!"

He got out of the car and continued walking west on I-70. As dawn began to creep up on the horizon behind him, Mitko noticed two horses tied in a grove of trees, and there was a small tent near a smoldering campfire. He quietly approached the tent and put his rifle to his shoulder before kicking down the tent poles. The tent collapsed and Mitko could see two figures lying inside.

"Get out here right now," Mitko called out. "I have a rifle pointed at your head. Don't do anything stupid!"

Tad North awoke from someone shouting, and then nearly panicked as he felt the weight of the tent on top of him. He fought his way to the opening and unzipped it, only to find himself staring into the barrel of a gun held by a Coalition soldier. He ducked back inside and shouted, "Hey, don't shoot!"

David stirred in his bag at the sound of his father's voice, and

Tad held him down. "There's a gunman out there, and he's definitely not one of us."

"Get out of the tent," Mitko demanded. "You have five seconds before I shoot you both."

The Norths quickly complied, standing in their socks in the snow. They were still a little groggy and could hardly believe what they had gotten themselves into. How had the Coalition army made it through that awful storm?

Mitko sized up his two captives, smiling inwardly. Both men were clean cut and had a light in their eyes that basically screamed "Latter-day Saint." He even suspected they were father and son. But he had to keep the upper hand if he was going to accomplish what the Lord had in mind.

Mitko pointed the gun at David and directed him to sit in the snow and stay quiet. Then he turned his attention to Tad. "If you answer my questions truthfully, I will spare you. But if I sense that you're lying, I won't hesitate to kill you. Do you understand?"

Tad nodded and glanced nervously at David, truly wondering if he would live much longer. This Coalition soldier seemed a little off his rocker.

"Are you alone, or with a group?" Mitko asked.

"We have friends nearby," Tad said, not wanting to be too specific.

"Are they Mormons?" Mitko asked.

Tad looked curiously at him. "What does that matter?"

Mitko shook the rifle at Tad. "Answer me! What religion do you belong to?"

"We are Latter-day Saints—or as you said, Mormons."

Mitko rejoiced inside, but he kept a stern face. "Are you part of an army?"

Tad and David again glanced at each other, and Mitko shouted, "Answer me!"

"Yes."

"Where is your army?"

"A few miles to the west, on the outskirts of Denver."

Mitko was quiet for several seconds, then with his rifle still at his shoulder, he asked, "Would you believe me if I told you I'm an elder in the LDS Church?"

Tad was stunned. "What kind of question is that?"

Mitko smiled a little as tears came to his eyes. After all of these years alone in the gospel, he was finally among his brethren again.

Tad was really confused. "Are you saying you're a Mormon? How is that even possible?"

Mitko nodded. "Yes, I'm LDS. My name is Mitko Petrov. I served a mission here in the United States before returning to my home in Bulgaria. I was later given little choice but to join the Coalition forces. It has been difficult, but I'm beginning to see the Lord's hand in it."

Tad was still wary. "I want to believe you, but what if you're setting us up? Anyone could make up those basic facts."

"I understand your worry, but we don't have much time," Mitko said. "I know it is the Lord's will that I found you. I have information that I need to share with your leaders. The Coalition forces aren't far behind me. They're exhausted and weak, but they are getting desperate to reach Denver."

Tad was torn inside. If this soldier was telling the truth, the information he possessed could save the lives of thousands of Saints. But if he was lying and they took him into their camp, he could somehow lead the Coalition forces straight to them.

David suddenly spoke up. "To prove that you are LDS, let's have you answer a few questions."

Mitko nodded. "Fair enough."

"Tell us the members of the First Presidency."

Mitko raised his eyebrows. "What kind of test is this?"

David shrugged. "Well, I'm pretty sure an imposter wouldn't even know what the First Presidency is, much less be able to tell us who is in it."

"Okay, but cut me a little slack, since I've been out of contact with the Church for quite a while."

"Just answer the question," Tad said.

Mitko pondered for a moment. "I had been home from my mission for a while when we received the news that President Gordon B. Hinckley had passed away. The new First Presidency consisted of President Thomas S. Monson, with Henry B. Eyring and Dieter F. Uchtdorf serving as his counselors. The Saints in Bulgaria loved them all, but they were really excited to have President Uchtdorf in the First Presidency, since we feel he's from the 'Old Country' like us. Of course, I have no idea what has happened during the past few years, but those men were in the First Presidency when I joined the Coalition army and lost contact with the Church."

David was impressed. "I would say he passed the test."

"I don't know . . ." Tad said.

Mitko gave him an impatient glare. "Hey, who has the gun here? Shouldn't I be the one who is being cautious?"

"I suppose so."

"How about this," Mitko said. "The First Vision was in 1820. The Church was restored in 1830. Joseph Smith was killed in 1844. Brigham Young said 'This is the place' in 1847. The Manifesto against polygamy was issued in 1890. Are you satisfied yet?"

"All right," Tad said with smile.

"Then put your boots on and let's get to your camp," Mitko said. "We don't have time to waste."

They quickly loaded up their gear and readied their horses, and in a final show of trust, Mitko handed the rifle to Tad before climbing up behind David on his horse. "By the way, what are your names?"

"I'm David North, and the slightly paranoid man over there is my father Tad."

Mitko smiled. "It's a pleasure to meet you. It has been too long since I've been with other priesthood brethren."

"Well, you're about to meet thousands of them. Our army is called the Elders of Israel, and they're all priesthood holders."

Mitko felt a stirring in his chest, hardly believing how everything was piecing together. "I can't wait to meet them."

They guided the horses back onto the freeway and then moved along swiftly, only stopping to tell the other pairs of lookouts in the communities along the way what was happening and that the Coalition soldiers weren't far behind.

They rode with urgency throughout the day, even switching horses with the final lookouts so that they could reach Elder Smith as soon as possible.

Mitko's backside and legs were definitely sore as they galloped the final stretch of road toward the main camp. He was in pain, but he grinned as he remembered that just a few days earlier he had envisioned himself as an impatient racehorse eager to start the Kentucky Derby. It was safe to say he had now definitely embarked on that race.

Chapter 23

An hour later Mitko found himself in a Church meetinghouse in the Denver suburb of Aurora. The leaders of the Elders of Israel were headquartered there, and they were surprised when Tad and David showed up with a Coalition soldier.

Tad quickly explained to them how Mitko had found them that morning, and Mitko then told his story to the leaders. As he was doing so, one of the leaders called up Mitko's membership record through the Church satellite system, and it confirmed everything he was saying.

After Mitko shared his story, Elder Smith took him into a separate room, where the apostle kindly yet firmly interviewed him. Elder Smith prayed fervently while doing so that he would be able to detect any deception on Mitko's part, and within five minutes he felt the confirmation from the Spirit that Mitko was telling the truth.

When they emerged from the room, the apostle said to the others, "This young man has no allegiance to the Coalition and only joined because he didn't have any other options. In fact, I believe he was led here by the Lord and will be a valuable asset for us. So let's listen to any ideas he may have."

They moved to the Relief Society room and arranged the chairs in a big circle. Mitko and Elder Smith sat together, while the other leaders completed the circle. Once the leaders were settled, Elder Smith motioned for Mitko to speak.

"Most of you already know my basic story, but I want to tell you more about the army you will be facing," Mitko said. "Two weeks ago they were very strong and almost overconfident. But they weren't prepared for the journey across Kansas. This latest snowstorm was a disaster for them, and I know it was an act of God that was intended to slow them down. Many of the soldiers are now weakened, cold, and nearly ready to give up."

One of the men asked, "What are their plans? Do they even know we are here?"

"Their plans are to reach Denver, rest up, then begin to spread out along the different freeways and finish off anyone who is still living here," Mitko said. "They have no idea that there are tens of thousands of Latter-day Saints here in the mountains. I had a hunch you were here, but I never told anyone. The Coalition has been able to track the rest of the U.S. citizens through their chip implants and eliminate them, but since hardly any of the Saints received the chip, the computers only show a few hundred people still living in the Rocky Mountains. Those are the people they intend to track down and kill. So in the minds of the Coalition leaders, this war is basically over, with just a little mop-up duty."

The room went silent. It hadn't dawned on the Church leaders that the Coalition didn't know they were there. It could give them the upper hand.

Elder Smith asked, "How many soldiers does the Coalition have? We received reports that there were as many as 20,000 in Kansas City. That's more than double our number."

Mitko nodded. "The Coalition left Kansas City with 15,000 soldiers, but the cold weather and sickness during the past week has been brutal on them. I'd say they're down to around half that number."

"Well, maybe this will be a fair fight after all," Elder Smith said hopefully.

"Don't underestimate them, though," Mitko said. "They're still as blood-thirsty and ruthless as ever. I'm sure the elders don't have that type of killer instinct. If we fight them head-to-head, it could get ugly for us."

"It's interesting that you would say that, because all along we have felt prompted to avoid such a battle," the apostle said. "The prophet has felt all along that this army would be like the Mormon Battalion with only a few lives lost, but I don't see how we can defeat them without a confrontation. Do you have any suggestions? Is there a weakness we can exploit?"

Mitko pondered for a moment, then remembered his strange dream from the night before. "We definitely need to use a strategy, and maybe this is part of the Lord's plan," he said. "Last night I dreamed I was one of Helaman's stripling warriors in the Book of Mormon, and we were being pursued by a Lamanite army. But little did the Lamanites know we were leading them straight into a trap."

Elder Smith nodded. "I think you're describing Alma 56."

"I'll trust you on that," Mitko said with a grin. "But I believe I had this dream for a reason, because such a plan is our best chance. The Nephites didn't lose many men in that battle, and we shouldn't have to either."

"Yes, I like the sound of it," Elder Smith said. "But how could we pull off something like that in such a short amount of time?"

Tad suddenly had an idea pop into his head, and he asked for a map of downtown Denver. He had visited the city several times for sporting events, even as recently as two years earlier when the Salt Lake Gladiatorzz had played the Denver Demons in the Conquest League.

Tad opened up the map and had David help him hold it against the wall. He pointed to a certain spot. "We are right here, not far from where I-70 joins East Colfax Road, the street that leads right into downtown Denver."

Tad could tell he had their attention, and he quickly continued, "David and other young soldiers could be the bait, just like Helaman's stripling warriors were. They could lead the Coalition army into downtown Denver. Getting the Coalition soldiers onto Colfax Road will be like forcing them into a funnel."

"Where would we lead them?" Elder Smith asked. Tad pointed on the map to a small oval along the South Platte River.

"Straight into our trap—Mile High Stadium," he said. "We'll have 1,000 of our best marksmen situated along the top of the stadium, ready to pick off the Coalition soldiers as they come into range on the road below. Then we'll have our remaining soldiers waiting inside the stadium to take care of anyone else. Hopefully they'll see their situation and even surrender."

Tad smiled. He had loved the Denver Broncos as a young man and had watched them whenever they were on TV. The Broncos had even won two Super Bowls. But he knew those victories couldn't compare to the epic battle the Elders of Israel were about to face.

Chapter 24

Two days later the final lookout pair had returned to the base camp outside of Denver. They said the Coalition army was marching forward quickly and would be there by late afternoon.

"Spread the word," Elder Smith said. "Get everyone in their places. It's time to put the plan into motion."

The apostle and a few other leaders were going to stay hidden in the meetinghouse. Meanwhile, more than 7,000 elders had already marched to downtown Denver, where they were stationed either along the top rows of Mile High Stadium or hiding inside it. Tad and Mitko were there among them, and they had more than enough ammunition to end the battle quickly. It would all depend on the bait luring the Coalition into their trap.

David was part of that bait—roughly 1,000 healthy, athletic young men under the age of 21 who were waiting on East Colfax Road. They were positioned at a curve in the road so that the Coalition army would spot them, but then they could quickly run ahead and hopefully stay out of rifle range. They had chosen to not carry any weapons, fearing that the extra weight would slow them down.

There was one young man about 200 yards behind them, watching for the army. He soon came running toward them. "Here they come!" he shouted, and David's heart nearly leapt out of his chest. The group stood poised to run, but they knew they had to let the Coalition soldiers get a good look at them first.

The army came into view, and then two soldiers seemed to spot them at the same time. The army halted and for an agonizing second both groups stared at each other. Then one of the Coalition soldiers put a rifle to his shoulder and fired. A young man named Andy who was five feet from David dropped to the ground. "I'm hit," he screamed as blood began to ooze from his upper right arm.

"Run!" David shouted to the group, and then he rushed to Andy's side and threw his arm around his waist. "Get up. You're coming with us."

The group's initial positioning worked out well, because within a few seconds the sprinting elders had rounded the curve and were out of sight from the army. David and another elder helped Andy move away from the road and hide under a bush. David ripped off part of his shirt and tied a tourniquet just above the bullet wound, then asked the other elder to stay with Andy.

"When their soldiers have passed by, you two need to go back to the meetinghouse," David said. "They'll take care of you there."

The pair agreed, and then David took off running to catch up with the group. He glanced back and spotted the soldiers coming around the bend. "Holy heck, that's too close," he said as his legs kicked into overdrive.

When the Coalition forces first saw the group of elders standing in the road ahead of them, some of the soldiers actually thought it must be an illusion. But they fired a rifle in that direction, and someone actually fell down.

The Coalition soldiers began pursuing the group, hoping to capture at least one of them so they could find out where their food was stored. It hadn't even crossed the soldiers' minds that they were chasing anything but a band of lawless young men who had banded together in the chaotic fall of the United States. They had encountered similar groups in the eastern half of the country and it always led to food.

However, the chase had now gone for several miles, past several subdivisions and toward Denver's skyscrapers. Many of the

Coalition soldiers were ready to give up the chase, but their leaders wouldn't let them stop, reasoning that there was a better chance of finding food and suitable shelter in the downtown area anyway.

David's group had managed to stay just far enough ahead of the army that although additional rifle shots had been fired in their direction, no one had been hit. At one point the group crossed an overpass, and David looked back at the thousands of soldiers about 500 yards behind them. It was terrifying, but as he turned forward again, he could see Mile High Stadium up ahead.

"We're almost there!" he shouted to the group of young elders, and they gathered up their remaining energy for a sprint to the stadium.

Mitko was leaning over a railing at the top of the stadium, watching David's group carefully. The Coalition soldiers seemed to figure out the group was heading for the stadium, and they gave one final sprint, but it looked like the elders were barely going to make it safely inside. The scheme had worked just as they had planned.

Mitko turned to watch Commander Whitney, the leader of the sharpshooters. The commander had served as a Marine for several years and had everyone's respect.

"Just a couple minutes more," Commander Whitney called out to the men. "Don't shoot until I tell you to."

Mitko had been torn inside about whether to be part of the sharpshooters. He finally decided not to participate. He had never shot an American, and although he had caused what his countrymen were about to experience, he couldn't shoot one of them, either. His heart ached as he started down the steps to meet David and the other elders.

More than a thousand of the Elders of Israel were now side by side along the top of the stadium's east side. Each one had his rifle at his shoulder and a Coalition soldier on the highway below selected as his first target.

"Fire!" Commander Whitney shouted when the Coalition soldiers were within fifty yards of the stadium, and the sound of gunfire filled the air. Within half a minute, thousands of Coalition soldiers had been either killed or severely wounded. As they fell, another wave of Coalition soldiers rushed forward, unsure what was happening, and they were also gunned down.

It was a horrendous mismatch, and the Coalition soldiers were so overwhelmed they didn't even know where to fire their guns. Many of the remaining soldiers panicked and jumped into the nearby South Platte River, but it was swollen from spring runoff and they quickly disappeared in the frigid water.

Others had vowed to never be taken alive, and so as the situation became obvious, many took their own lives.

"Cease fire!" Commander Whitney called out after a mere two minutes of carnage.

The elders held their weapons and watched the ground below, but there was no movement among the Coalition soldiers. Within a few minutes all of the elders were gathered on the ground level of the stadium, and Commander Whitney spoke to them.

"We owe this victory to the Lord," he said. "Our leaders were inspired how to best handle the Coalition forces, and fortunately it all worked out in our favor. We have preserved our liberty."

One of the soldiers started to clap, but Commander Whitney was on him like a tiger. "There's no reason to celebrate," he shouted. "We just sent thousands of our brothers to the Spirit World, and they weren't prepared for it. This is a day of mourning. Now let's go out there and see if there are any survivors. Check each body for a pulse. If you find someone alive, bring him into the stadium to receive medical attention. Mitko, please be there to talk to them if they regain consciousness."

As the elders walked outside, the bodies were more numerous than they had anticipated. Commander Whitney decided they had only one option to humanely deal with the situation.

"We can't just leave their bodies lying out in the open, but the ground is still too frozen to dig proper graves," he said. "We need to borrow from the book of Alma once again. Place their bodies in the river, like Alma did with the Lamanites at the River Sidon."

The elders worked throughout the night on their unpleasant task, and they found two dozen Coalition soldiers who were still alive. Some regained consciousness, and Mitko talked to each one as their wounds were treated. Most of them were initially hostile, but they calmed down as Mitko explained that if they would surrender peacefully, they would be treated well and even be allowed to stay with their group if they wanted.

After talking to each of the survivors, Mitko walked to a dark corner of the stadium. He leaned against a wall and began shaking and crying. The stress of the past few days had been almost unbearable, but he knew he had made the right decision and that the Lord had been with him.

As he reflected back on his life, he realized all of his experiences had been pointing to this day when he would help the Elders of Israel defend their land. Now he would teach the gospel to the surviving Coalition soldiers if they wanted to listen to him.

Mitko finally smiled. Although the rest of the world didn't know it yet, the war in America was over.

Chapter 25

The next morning in Salina, President Johnson opened his Church-issued laptop and noticed there was an urgent message for him. He opened up the message and could hardly believe it.

"Woohoo! The war's over!" he shouted, and the members of his household rushed into the room. He stood up and gave his wife a hug, then he read the message to them that had been sent to stake presidents across the world from the First Presidency.

Dear brethren,

The war in America is over!

Elder Smith is in Denver and reports that through careful planning and perseverance, the Elders of Israel have defeated the remaining Coalition forces. The hand of the Lord was evident in the decisions that were made, and the elders suffered very few casualties.

For now, stay in your current location. Within a short time each stake will be instructed concerning future movements.

Please make this a day of gladness and gratitude among the members in your stake. It is truly a momentous day that we will long remember.

The news quickly spread throughout Salina, and the people poured out of their homes into the streets. It seemed as though a horrible cloud had suddenly lifted from the earth. Nearly every family in Salina was directly connected to the Elders of Israel, and the news that there were few casualties was a great relief.

Emma clung to Charles and Leah, hardly able to contain her emotions. There was no word on whether Tad or David had survived, but Emma was comforted in the fact the war was over. "Hopefully our family will be together again soon," she told the children.

President Johnson announced that there would be a feast that evening at the stake center, and Emma threw herself into the preparations. Doug and Becky assured her that if anything had happened to Tad or David, the Church leaders would have let her know.

Partway through the meal, President Johnson went to the stage and said he had received another message from the First Presidency. A hush fell over the group as he read, "*We request that the Saints currently in Salina, Utah, prepare immediately to journey to Denver, where your soldiers will be waiting for you. We are happy to report that none of your elders were killed in the battle.*"

A spontaneous cheer erupted, and President Johnson added, "Let's plan on leaving at 8 a.m. Now we can really celebrate!"

Emma exploded in tears. "Thank thee, Heavenly Father, for watching over them," she cried as her family members gathered around her.

She noticed Jonas Fernelius standing nearby, and she gave him a hug, too. "Isn't that great news?" she asked him. I can't wait for you to meet Tad. I think you too are going to be great friends."

Jonas gave a faint smile. "Yes, I can't wait to see him."

Inwardly, Jonas was a bit nervous. He had purposely changed his look from when he was a CCA agent. The shaved head and goatee had been replaced with a full head of hair and a clean-shaven face. There was little chance Tad would recognize him. He had decided if Tad really needed to know who he really was, it would be Jonas' decision and no one else's.

The Saints left Salina right on time and began their journey across the barren stretch of I-70 through central Utah. But they were energized and maintained a steady pace. Within a week they had reached the city of Grand Junction, Colorado.

Later that night, they were approached by a group of men. President Johnson had the high priests rush forward, but soon they saw familiar faces. The Manti Men had returned to their families.

Emma rushed into Tad's arms, and David joined them. It was a wonderful reunion for everyone. Once the hugs and kisses had calmed down, President Johnson asked Tad, "Why are you here? How did you even know where to find us?"

Tad shrugged. "We finished our duties in Denver and Elder Smith let us know that you were likely going to travel along I-70 to join us. So we asked permission to meet you. I'm glad we did. The earthquake has turned the freeway into a mess, but we cleared it as we traveled along. You're actually farther along than we thought you would be."

"That's what happens when you get driven out of Manti," President Johnson said. Tad looked shocked, and President Johnson said, "Let's gather all of the Manti Men around and we'll tell you about it. We've had our own share of excitement while you've been gone."

The next hour turned into a mini-testimony meeting as the Saints told the elders about their narrow escape from Sherem's army. Richard Dalton stood and told what he had discovered in Birdseye, and the Manti Men sat there slightly stunned.

"Wow, that would've been a real disaster if we had returned to find you all dead," Tad said, a bit sick to his stomach.

"We were being watched over," Doug said. "The Lord sent a good man to warn us, Jonas Ferguson."

The Saints began to applaud, and Doug introduced Jonas to the Manti Men, who expressed sincere gratitude as they were told how Jonas had saved their lives.

President Johnson stepped forward and put his arm around Jonas' shoulder. "Actually, Jonas has been meeting with me the past couple of weeks, and he has an announcement to make."

Jonas nodded. "Through everyone's example, I became curious

about the church. President Johnson has served as my own personal missionary, and I am going to be baptized into the Church soon."

There's nothing more exciting to Mormons than when someone chooses to join the Church, and this news was met with wild applause. Their hero was going to become one of them!

All of this good news sparked a spontaneous party. All that was missing was the green Jello and the cultural hall. The Saints gathered around two large bonfires and danced and talked until almost midnight. Emma was essentially glued to Tad all night. As angry as she had been at him when he had received the chip, she now felt closer to him than she ever had.

David was thrilled to be back among his siblings, and the three of them spent the night telling each other about their experiences. Leah was starstruck as she listened to David tell about how he had helped lead the Coalition soldiers into the trap at Mile High Stadium. The past few months had been unbelievable, yet here they were, back together as a family.

As midnight approached, President Johnson called out, "I know we won't get much sleep tonight, but let's get in our sleeping bags and quiet down. I'll offer a closing prayer on the evening." He then gave a powerful prayer in which he thanked the Lord for many things, including the miraculous preservation of their soldiers. Then he paused before saying, "I don't dare ask for anything this night. Thy blessings have been so bountiful unto us." Then he closed the prayer, and the entire group gave a heartfelt "Amen."

A couple of days later as the Manti group walked to Denver, Jonas saw Tad walking alone. He caught up to him and said, "As you know, I am planning on being baptized, and President Johnson has taught me about repentance. So I need to start with you and give a huge apology."

Tad was taken aback. "Why? You saved my family from that band of criminals. I'll always be grateful to you."

Jonas nodded slowly. "I appreciate that, but look carefully at my face. Jonas put his hands across his forehead, hiding his shaggy hair. "Now add a goatee."

Tad looked for a moment, but still didn't catch on. Finally Jonas said, "Also, my real last name isn't Ferguson. It's Fernelius."

The name alone made Tad cringe and take a step backward.

Jonas nodded slowly. "That's the response I expected."

Tad was nearly having a panic attack. Here stood the one man on earth he truly hated—and feared. "I don't believe my eyes," he said, completely stunned.

Jonas smiled slightly. "I can hardly believe it myself. All I can do is start at the beginning, when you escaped, and tell you how everything unfolded." He shook his head and rubbed his eyes. "Sheesh, I've been imagining this conversation for weeks, but now I can hardly get the words out. I guess I'll start with a question. Where were you hiding after you left the locker room of the Lincoln Point swimming pool?"

"I was up on West Mountain. I watched you the day you came and searched the locker room."

"I knew it! I was going to get a tracking dog that same week, but then the earthquake hit. It probably saved your life, because at that point I might have killed you with my bare hands."

Tad's eyes got big. "You're over that now, right?"

Jonas laughed. "Yes. But your antics got me fired." He then went on to explain his downward spiral after that, until he had hooked up with Sherem as a bodyguard.

Tad pondered for a moment. "Sherem . . . Sherem! You mean Larry Campbell?"

"Exactly. He hates you for turning down his offer to be in his bishopric."

Tad shook his head. "I can't believe that nutcase is still around—and living in the State Capitol!"

Jonas then got serious. "There's one other person I need to tell you about. Ken Turner."

"Oh, no. Did he get mixed up with Sherem too?"

"Yes, and he was the one leading the army that was going to

attack Manti," Jonas said with pain in his eyes. "He told me all about your family, and how I could infiltrate them. He was the mastermind behind the whole attack."

Tad's blood began to boil. "Ken sold his soul for money. That's someone I will have a hard time ever forgiving. It's because of him that I got the government chip in the first place."

"Well, you might as well forgive him, because he's dead."

"What? Are you sure?"

"After the army invaded Manti but didn't find any Saints, they headed toward Spanish Fork Canyon. Somewhere along the way there was a mutiny, and Sherem's men took care of Ken for you. Richard Dalton found him hanging from a tree."

The news hit Tad harder than he thought it would. "Wow, Ken is dead. I would hate to be him right now in the Spirit World."

They were silent for a moment, then Tad tried to lighten the mood. "I just want to make sure of one thing—you're not still planning on arresting me, are you?" he asked half-seriously.

Jonas laughed. "I think that arrest warrant vanished about the same time the government did." He paused for a moment. "By the way, I want you to know that only President Johnson is aware we have a connection. I have told him about my past—and my involvement with you. But no one else knows about it, and if you agree, I'd like to keep it that way and start with a clean slate. In fact, I now consider myself Jonas Ferguson, and that's how I want to be known. I'm putting my old identity in the past. But both President Johnson and I felt that in order to make my repentance complete, I needed to speak to you."

"I understand."

So here goes," Jonas said. "I'm so very sorry for how I treated you. Will you forgive me?"

Tad was on a roller coaster of emotions. Here stood the man who had hunted him like a dog and made him fear he would never see his family again. But slowly the words came out that he never expected to say. "I forgive you . . . with all of my heart."

Both men began to weep, and then they embraced—two bitter

foes were on their way to a solid friendship. Jonas pulled back and said, "There is just one more thing. Would you be willing to baptize me?"

Tad was nearly overcome by the request, but he said, "I would be honored."

Two days later on a beautiful Sunday morning, Jonas and Tad stepped into slow-moving portion of a very frigid Colorado River. They wore white shirts and blue jeans, since no one had brought along white pants, and hundreds of people stood on the bank as Tad said the baptismal prayer and lowered Jonas into the water. Jonas popped back up with a huge grin on his face, and the men slapped each other on the back before scampering to dry land.

After they had changed into dry clothes, President Johnson confirmed Jonas a member of the Church, and then the whole group gathered to shake Jonas' hand.

As they were walking up the hill, President Johnson pulled Tad aside and said, "Great job—on both counts. I know that forgiving Jonas couldn't have been easy, but it has set you both free. It's wonderful to see you becoming the man I always knew was inside of you—and the kind of man your beautiful wife Emma deserves."

Chapter 26

Josh Brown had received the same message from the First Presidency that President Johnson did, and he had the same euphoric reaction about the war being over. But before he shared the news with anyone, he wanted a bit more clarification. The Saints in Hopiland knew they only had one destination ahead of them—Missouri. So it wouldn't help matters very much if he didn't have a departure date.

Elder Smith had told him to contact him directly on any matters related to the Guatemalan Saints, and as a member of the First Quorum of the Seventy, Josh had access to Elder Smith's direct e-mail address. Josh quickly fired off a message asking the apostle what the next step should be for his group, and he waited anxiously all day for a reply. Late in the evening it finally came.

"Elder Brown, your long wait in the desert is finally over," the apostle responded. "Bring those Saints to Missouri immediately!"

Josh knew it was too late in the evening to get everyone excited about leaving, but he located Mathoni and told him the news. The Nephite had returned from meeting with the modern apostles the previous week, and had spent all of his time secretly setting up water storage areas all along I-40 into New Mexico and Texas, so Josh had expected Mathoni to already have heard the news, but he hadn't.

"That's wonderful," Mathoni said. "I know the prophet felt confident that everything would go well, but it is a relief to know the war is over. I'll get to work tonight on loading food into the handcarts."

"What about the bus?" Josh asked. "Will we load it too?"

Mathoni shook his head. "There is so much going on right now that the prophet won't have time to translate the plates. Besides, the bus is so encased under those rocks that the plates will be safe for a long time. Once the holy temple in Zion is well-underway, you and I will return for the bus."

Mathoni said it matter-of-factly, but Josh marveled at what his friend had just hinted about. Josh was going to see the temple in New Jerusalem being built, as well as transport sacred records there! It was almost too much to comprehend. But Mathoni was right. There was much to do before the plates needed to be retrieved.

The next morning Josh made the announcement to the entire group, and everyone was thrilled, especially Kim. She had still been secretly hoping her twins would be born in New Jerusalem, and now it looked like it was going to happen.

Josh and Mathoni met with the Hopi and Guatemalan leaders, and their route was mapped out. They would leave Hopiland and travel east on I-40 all the way to Oklahoma City. From that point the group would go north on I-35 to Wichita, Kansas, and then follow the same freeway northeast across the state straight to Kansas City.

Some of the leaders were worried about having someone who would recognize landmarks and guide them on the right way. "We have maps, but who knows if there are still road signs," one leader said. "For all we know, they've been burned for firewood."

Josh nodded. "That is a valid concern, but I lived in the Midwest for many years, and my wife and I traveled these same roads that we will be taking. When Elder Smith called me to this position, he said that part of the reason I had received the calling was because I knew the way to Missouri. So I might not be worth much else, but I think I can get us there."

The leaders laughed at his self-depreciation, because they knew it wasn't true. Each one of them had grown to love and respect their

"Little White Brother" as they privately called him. They knew his only goal was to serve them and help them in any way that he could. And his wife was right there with him in terms of respect and honor. In the leaders' eyes, Josh and Kim were just a little bit lower than the "Great White Brother" that they all revered.

After the meeting, Josh spoke with Mathoni privately. "My only worry is crossing Texas," he said. "Not too long ago there were bands of uncivilized people battling each other throughout that area. That's the whole reason we diverted to Arizona."

"I know, but I checked it out while I was setting up the water storages, and everyone is gone," Mathoni said. "Maybe that group of Coalition soldiers that left Lake Powell finished them off, but we shouldn't have any interference."

"I'm relieved to hear that."

Mathoni smiled and clasped his friend's shoulder. "By the way, you truly are a great leader, Josh. I've known a lot of them through the centuries, and you're right there at the top."

Josh was touched by Mathoni's words. "I don't quite know what to say. All I'm trying to do is the Lord's will."

"Exactly," Mathoni said. "That's what I'm saying. Just keep it up. I promise you that all of this stress and effort is going to be worth it for these Saints. It almost makes me wish I was mortal again! Well, not really, but life in Zion is going to be wonderful for them—and for you."

Chapter 27

The Manti Saints soon arrived at the Denver Temple, located several miles south of the downtown area. The elders had made certain to stay clear of Mile High Stadium, where the memories of the final battle with the Coalition soldiers were still too fresh on their minds.

Elder Smith greeted them warmly, and Tad introduced the group to Mitko Petrov, who had played such a key role in the victory. That afternoon President Johnson met privately with Elder Smith and asked what lay ahead. "There's a big surprise coming soon," the apostle said. "You'll just have to wait and see like everyone else!"

The next evening as the Saints were gathering for dinner on the temple grounds, they noticed several wagons had entered through the main gate. The wagons pulled to a stop near the crowd, and to everyone's delight several of the apostles climbed out of the first wagon. They waved to the crowd, then walked toward the second wagon, where they assisted the two counselors in the First Presidency to exit their wagon.

Then to everyone's surprise, the prophet himself could be seen sitting in the back of the wagon. The crowd cheered as the prophet was helped into a wheelchair and pushed toward the temple. He waved happily to everyone and called out, "That ride didn't sit too well on my old bones. Let me rest for a few minutes, then we'll have a great meeting. Enjoy your meal!"

The Saints buzzed with excitement at the prospect of hearing from the prophet. The other apostles mingled with the Saints, and meals were quickly prepared for them as well.

David had never seen the prophet in person, and he was awestruck. "I thought the prophet wasn't feeling well enough to leave Rexburg," he told Emma.

"You can't ever count him out," she said with a shrug. "He just keeps surprising us with what he's able to do!"

A half hour later the prophet appeared at the temple door, and several of the apostles helped lift his wheelchair onto a small stage so that everyone could see him better. He was also handed a microphone that was connected to an outdoor sound system.

The prophet gazed out at the thousands of Saints that had gathered near the front of the temple. The tables had been moved, and rows of chairs were in place, but many hundreds more were either sitting on the ground or standing toward the back of the crowd.

"Let me be the first to say what a beautiful sight you are," the prophet said in a strong voice. "I sense a holiness about you—this is a people that has been tried, tested, and refined during the past year. Please think back to last spring when the invitation was issued to gather to the mountain camps. You had many LDS friends, neighbors and family members who chose not to heed that invitation. But you did, and it has made all the difference, hasn't it?

"Then came the destruction of the national government, followed by a difficult winter, yet you stayed strong in the gospel. Many of you took part as soldiers in a crucial battle against the invading army, and you came out victorious.

"I want you to know the Lord is very pleased with you, and because of your faithfulness, this group will be among the first to return to Jackson County, Missouri and build New Jerusalem. That event is even at our doors."

The Saints could hardly contain their excitement, and Tad was weeping with joy, grateful that he hadn't thrown this opportunity away through his foolishness. He looked over at his new friend Jonas who also seemed deeply touched.

Someone called out, "So when will it be? Tomorrow?"

The crowd laughed nervously at the man's bold question, but the prophet smiled. "It won't be long, maybe even within a few days. There are other groups who have made great sacrifices and also deserve the privilege of entering Jackson County with us, particularly the Saints in Rexburg. They are making their way here right now and should arrive soon. In the meantime we need to prepare for our journey. Just like the early Saints who crossed the plains in wagons and handcarts, we will be doing the same.

"Thankfully we'll be traveling on the paved freeway known as Interstate 70. Our scouts tell us that the bridges are intact, so it hopefully will be a fairly smooth trip. I can't complain. Brigham Young arrived in the Salt Lake Valley in the back of a wagon, and I suppose that will probably be my means of transportation, too. But I must tell you, I have really been missing my black limousine!"

The Saints laughed, and a woman called out, "We were worried that your recent illness wouldn't allow you to be with us. How are you feeling?"

The prophet sat up a little straighter in his wheelchair. "I might be getting a little feeble, but do you really think I'd stay back in Rexburg and miss out on all of this fun? I'm going to make it to Missouri, or I'm going to die trying!"

Chapter 28

Following the meeting, the prophet invited each of the Saints to pass by and shake his hand. It was a long process, but Doug sensed what the prophet was doing. When the resurrected Savior appeared to the Nephites, he allowed each person to feel the wounds in his hands and in his side. In a similar manner, the prophet was allowing these Saints to have an experience that would stay with them throughout their lifetimes. Many people were weeping openly, and the Spirit was burning into their hearts the testimony of a living prophet.

The Daltons soon had their turn, and Doug felt a burning in his chest as the Lord's prophet greeted each of his children. Becky was holding little Daniel, and the prophet motioned for him.

"Oh, it's all right," Becky said. But the prophet motioned for the baby once again.

"This is my privilege," the prophet said. "The Spirit has testified to me that you are holding one of the Lord's great servants. His little body might not allow him to stay on earth much longer, but I assure you that his work in the kingdom has just begun."

Becky began to weep openly and handed her son to the prophet, who gazed intently into Daniel's eyes. "Yes, this child is greatly loved by the Savior, and so are his parents."

* * *

The next morning as the Saints were gathered for breakfast, Elder Smith took the microphone and announced, "The First Presidency has requested that the following brethren and their wives come right now to the temple chapel. Please bear with me. There are about 100 names." He began reading from the list, and Doug recognized many of them as faithful men he had gotten to know in Manti.

Elder Smith read several more names, then said, " . . . and finally, Doug Dalton. Please come forward now and join the First Presidency in the temple."

Doug was baffled about what could possibly be happening, but he and Becky left the kids with Emma and Tad, then entered the temple. As they entered the temple chapel, the First Presidency was seated on the stand, and the apostles filled the chapel's first pew. Doug watched the apostles and was pleased that they seemed rather relaxed about everything, despite the heavy responsibilities they carried.

There were actually only seven members of the Quorum of the Twelve present. Two apostles had been in Europe at the time of the Coalition invasion, and they had been directing the Church organization in Europe and Asia since that time. One had been in Australia and was helping the Saints there, and yet another one was serving in South America. Sadly, another apostle had passed away in Rexburg the previous month and had been buried there. The vacancy in the quorum had yet to be filled.

The couples filled the rest of the pews, and everyone was silent. There was no indication of why they were there. One of the apostles gave a brief opening prayer inviting the Spirit of the Lord to be with them, then the prophet wheeled himself alongside the pulpit with a microphone in hand.

"I am deeply honored to be here," he said. "This is a momentous occasion that is being enacted in temples across the world today. Over the past few weeks in the Rexburg Temple, the members of Quorum of the Twelve have pleaded with the Lord for inspiration—better said, direct revelation—on this matter."

He took a set of scriptures from his lap and said, "Let me read you some verses that were written by John the Beloved nearly 2,000 years ago. It is in Revelation 7:1-4 and reads:

"And after these things I saw four angels standing on the four corners of the earth, holding the four winds of the earth, that the wind should not blow on the earth, nor on the sea, nor on any tree.

"And I saw another angel ascending from the east, having the seal of the living God: and he cried with a loud voice to the four angels, to whom it was given to hurt the earth and the sea,

"Saying, Hurt not the earth, neither the sea, nor the trees, till we have sealed the servants of our God in their foreheads.

"And I heard the number of them which were sealed: and there were sealed an hundred and forty and four thousand of all the tribes of the children of Israel.

The prophet then turned in his scriptures to another passage and said, "This verse is Doctrine and Covenants 77:11, and it is in the form of a question from Joseph Smith to the Lord, who provides the answer. It reads:

"Q. What are we to understand by sealing the one hundred and forty-four thousand, out of all the tribes of Israel—twelve thousand out of every tribe?

"A. We are to understand that those who are sealed are high priests, ordained unto the holy order of God, to administer the everlasting gospel; for they are they who are ordained out of every nation, kindred, tongue, and people, by the angels to whom is given power over the nations of the earth, to bring as many as will come to the church of the Firstborn."

Several men in the congregation were beginning to figure out what the prophet's message was, and they weren't sure whether to be happy or sad.

The prophet raised his voice and said, "Dear brethren, you are now called to be part of this vast group of high priests—144,000 of you—who will search the earth for the pure in heart. This is the Lord's will. As the apostle John made clear, the angels are ready and waiting that will cause great destructions among the wicked, but the Lord in his mercy will not turn those angels loose until you have performed your labor of gathering the remaining righteous people to Zion."

The shock among the group was palatable. None of them had ever expected this calling. Finally one man raised his hand and asked, "Why are you issuing these callings now? Couldn't we wait until we reached Missouri and got Zion established?"

The prophet looked thoughtful. "I asked the Lord the same question. But the answer I received is that there is no time to waste. In fact, we expect you to leave as early as tomorrow. We'll let the spry, youthful elders do the backbreaking work of building the celestial city. We need your spiritual experience to gather the precious souls who are out there in the world with nowhere to turn."

Another man asked, "What about the rest of the 144,000 the scriptures mention? Have they all been called?"

"Thank you for mentioning that. As the scripture from the 77th section indicates, 12,000 high priests from each tribe are to be called. Each of you are from the tribe of Joseph, descended either through his sons Ephraim or Manasseh. Finding worthy servants from the other tribes was a bit more difficult, but over the past few years the Lord has seen fit to bring these souls into the Church.

"Through our Church database of patriarchal blessings, we were able to identify 12,000 worthy men from each of the other tribes. They are scattered throughout the world, and under the direction of the Quorums of the Seventy, they are also gathering at certain temples and being given this same assignment.

"A large number of the men are fairly new to the Church, and most have only been high priests for less than a year, but their zeal for missionary work makes them perfect for the calling. They are all worthy men who will serve faithfully, whether they are in Europe, South America, Asia, Africa, or on the islands of the sea. The work of the Lord will not be stopped."

Doug marveled at how all of the prophecies were meshing together to fulfill the word of the Lord.

The wives were beginning to understand what this meeting was all about, and they realized their husbands were about to leave for an extended period of time. The prophet noticed their concern.

"Dear sisters, I'm sorry you have yet another trial to endure," the prophet said. "Yes, you'll travel to Missouri without your husbands at your side. But I testify that you will feel buoyed up, and the blessings that are reserved for you in heaven are difficult to fathom. The Savior's Second Coming is fast approaching, and if we stay faithful for just a little longer, then all that the Lord has will be ours."

It was late when they departed the temple, so Doug and Becky held off sharing the news with the rest of the family until the next morning. The others were in shock, but they expressed their support of the calling.

Emma felt a tinge of sadness, because she knew one of her brother's greatest dreams was to join the Saints as they returned to New Jerusalem. "This means you won't be able to be with us when we reach Missouri."

"That's okay," Doug said. "I'm sure I'll get there someday. The important thing is to do whatever the Lord requires. This is truly a great honor that I could never have imagined, and I'm very humbled by it."

"Were you assigned a certain area?" Tad asked.

"No, but those of us who served missions in the United States have been asked to return to those areas first and check the meetinghouses to see if any Saints are gathered there. Then we should just follow the Spirit in finding the pure in heart."

Becky grimaced a little. "So you'll be going to New Jersey's inner cities? Oh, I'm a little nervous about that."

Doug chuckled. "So am I! It wasn't exactly the safest place when I served there twenty years ago. But like I said, I'm going to trust in the Lord to watch over me."

Becky wiped her eyes. "This is harder than I thought it would be, but I suppose it's my turn to sacrifice. I have felt so lucky to have you at my side during the past few months, but I've also felt a bit guilty because Emma endured so much without Tad there."

"You know we'll be here for you," Emma said. She gave Becky a confident look. "Hey, we got by just fine with only one man around. We can do it again."

Everyone smiled, but they knew Doug needed to depart. He hugged Becky tightly, then kissed his little children Justin and Heather. Finally he took baby Daniel in his arms and held him close, hoping to see him again in mortality. The prophet's words had made him wonder what lay ahead for his son.

Becky moved forward and took Daniel from him. "Everything will be all right," she told her husband. "Trust in the Lord."

Chapter 29

By the end of the day all of the 100 high priests had departed on their missions, and the Saints at the Denver Temple shifted into high gear getting everything prepared. The Rexburg group arrived three days later, and they were eager to keep on moving, so the prophet told everyone who was ready to plan on departing at noon the next day.

It was an amazing sight to see the Saints lined up behind the wagons of the First Presidency and the apostles. The line of handcarts circled around the entire temple grounds. At high noon, one of the apostles sounded a whistle and the procession began moving forward. Within a day they reached I-70, and then it was basically a straight shot all the way to Missouri. The snow from that final monstrous storm had long melted away, and the freeway looked like a silver ribbon leading to Zion.

Three weeks later, everyone awoke excitedly, knowing it could be the day the group actually crossed over into the state of Missouri. The First Presidency had asked everyone to stay on the Kansas side of the Missouri River until instructed otherwise. The initial plan was to cross the river and travel on to Independence where Joseph Smith had dedicated the site for New Jerusalem's temple many decades earlier.

But as the morning progressed, it looked less likely they would cross over that day. Storm clouds filled the sky, and there was a slight drizzle. David had been asked to help repair a squeaky handcart, but Tad, Emma, Charles and Leah joined other families down on the river bank, looking longingly across the river. The storm clouds still hovered overhead and the wind was picking up. "At least it won't be long now," Tad said. "If we don't go across today, we certainly will tomorrow."

The part of Kansas City they gazed upon looked fairly intact, with an occasional church steeple even punctuating the skyline, but there wasn't any sign of human life.

Leah buttoned up her blue hand-me-down coat and pulled the hood over her head. She was cold, and she kicked at the mud along the river bank. She had to admit that she was a little disappointed at the scene across the river. In her young mind, she had pictured New Jerusalem as already built—like the Land of Oz—and that she and her family would happily skip right up to the front door.

To fight off her disappointment, she said a little prayer in her heart. "Heavenly Father, is this really where New Jerusalem will be built?"

Suddenly the sun pierced through the clouds and brightly illuminated a part of the city. Everyone huddled together and pointed out the striking scene.

"Wow, that's amazing," Tad said. "I can't help but feel that's some sort of sign for us."

Leah stayed quiet, but she knew her prayer had been answered.

Soon afterward, thunderstorms rolled through the area, and the official word came that they would have to wait one more day.

During the night the storm passed, and the morning dawned under a bright blue sky. Although members of the Church had been living in Missouri for several years until they were summoned to gather prior to the Coalition invasion, the return of the Saints to Missouri to build New Jerusalem was a major historic event. The Church leaders wanted to make a symbolic gesture that showed the importance of this return to the Zion.

The word spread that the prophet planned to be the first one to cross over into Missouri. In accordance, the Church leaders wanted as many members of the Church as possible to witness it. They had arranged for one of the Saints who had once worked for BYUTV to record the key events of the next few days with a battery-operated handheld video camera. His recording would then be put on the Church network and broadcast directly to the temples across the world, as well as be preserved for future generations.

Everyone was encouraged to eat a hearty breakfast, because once the group got moving, they didn't plan to stop until they reached the temple site in Independence a few miles beyond the state line. So after the meal, the Saints began lining up with their handcarts on the designated road behind the bridge where the prophet's wagon would cross over the river into Missouri.

At 10 a.m., the familiar wagons of the First Presidency and the Quorum of the Twelve rolled to the front of the line. As millions of Saints watched around the world, the cameras panned the long line of Saints waiting along the highway. Then the camera focused on the prophet's wagon as it began moving across the bridge. At the bridge's halfway point above the river, there was a sign that indicated the state line, and there was even a line painted across the roadway. The plan was for the wagon to simply roll into Missouri and continue on to Independence.

To everyone's surprise, the wagon stopped ten feet short of the Missouri state line, and two of the apostles helped the aging prophet out of the wagon to the roadway. No one was quite sure what was happening.

The apostles steadied him at each elbow as he walked with his cane until he stood next to the painted line. The prophet motioned for the apostles to let go of his elbows, and then the Saints across the world collectively held their breath as their beloved leader carefully took three steps forward on those frail legs, crossing into Missouri.

The prophet then turned and raised his cane above his head. "We are home, my beloved Saints," he shouted. "Bless the name of the Lord. We are home."

The two apostles rushed forward to steady him, and the Saints across the world cried with joy as the Spirit testified to them that their prophet was indeed the Lord's chosen servant. No one could ever remember such a collective outpouring of the Spirit. Some Saints who were there on the bridge even claimed to have seen former Church presidents dressed in white standing within a few feet of the prophet, although they weren't recorded on the video footage.

Once the prophet was lifted back inside the wagon, the procession of Saints began journeying to the temple site in Independence. The prophet's wagon led the way down Truman Road before turning onto South River Boulevard and arriving at the temple lot. New Jerusalem would soon be a reality.

Tad and Emma pushed their handcart together in the long line of Saints, and they watched Leah skipping along ahead of them, absolutely carefree. Tad turned and kissed his wife's cheek. "Thank you for believing in me and not letting me miss this great day."

It took the Saints a couple of days to get settled in and around Independence. For the time being, the Saints took possession of existing homes and apartment complexes that were near the temple site, staying together with their previously organized groups.

A ceremony was scheduled at the temple lot on Sunday at noon to officially commence the building of Zion. Thousands of Saints gathered in a huge circle, and the Church's video team continued to record the events and broadcast them on the Church satellite system.

The apostles were seated on a small stand, and the prophet was seated at a podium. "Thank you for coming," he told the assembled crowd. "This is a pivotal point in the history of the Church. The Lord is pleased with how we have grown from six members in 1830 to the millions across the world today. But this is only the beginning. Zion will fill the earth in a miraculous way, and this is the center point. The marvelous temple that will be built on this spot will astound the world, and all nations will flow unto it."

The prophet opened his scriptures and said, "The Lord has seen this day, and even told Joseph Smith about it. I will now quote D&C 84:1-4:

"A revelation of Jesus Christ unto his servant Joseph Smith, Jun., and six elders, as they united their hearts and lifted their voices on high.

"Yea, the word of the Lord concerning his church, established in the last days for the restoration of his people, as he has spoken by the mouth of his prophets, and for the gathering of his saints to stand upon Mount Zion, which shall be the city of New Jerusalem.

"Which city shall be built, beginning at the temple lot, which is appointed by the finger of the Lord, in the western boundaries of the State of Missouri, and dedicated by the hand of Joseph Smith, Jun., and others with whom the Lord was well pleased.

"Verily this is the word of the Lord, that the city New Jerusalem shall be built by the gathering of the saints, beginning at this place, even the place of the temple, which temple shall be reared in this generation."

The prophet closed his scriptures and said, "On this day—on the very ground that was dedicated by Joseph Smith—we will fulfill the word of the Lord. The time has come to break ground for our holy temple. Our apostles will do the honors." Then he paused before saying with a smile, "I think I'll just watch."

At that point the prophet's two counselors stood and moved to a patch of dirt that had been smoothed over. Each member of the First Presidency took a shovel and turned over the soil. They were followed by the seven apostles in attendance, who stood side by side and removed a shovelful of dirt, creating a small furrow.

The apostles then walked to a spot where a 12-foot-long log rested on the ground. The apostles lifted it in unison, put it on their shoulders, and walked slowly back to the furrow they had dug in the ground. They carefully lowered the log into the furrow, and then solemnly turned toward the prophet.

The prophet nodded his approval, and said, "From this center point we shall build a celestial city that will stand through the Millennium and into the eternities."

He asked the apostles to return to their seats, and then he addressed the worldwide audience. "As this city grows, some of you will be invited to move here, while most of you will be asked to stay in your current locations, building your own cities of Zion with your temple as the center point. Our beloved prophet Joseph spoke of the day when Zion would fill both North and South America, and the time has come to fulfill that marvelous prophecy.

"Although the war here in America has ended, there will always be turmoil in the world, and it will continue to increase as the Second Coming grows nearer. But I feel in my heart that there will be ways for visitors to come to this city. Just as millions of Saints visited Temple Square in Salt Lake City, opportunities will come for Saints from across the globe to visit here and worship in the magnificent temple that we have begun today.

"But most importantly, now is the time, more than ever, to follow your Savior. Create a spirit of cooperation in your temple cities and follow your local leaders as they direct you in building your own portion of Zion. Under the direction of the Great Architect, our beloved Savior, Zion will arise as a powerful force throughout the earth. I testify that Jesus Christ is directing this work, and I say these things in his holy name, Amen."

The next two weeks were filled with excitement as the Church leaders mapped out New Jerusalem, based on the original street pattern Joseph Smith had drawn up in the 1830s, as well as additions the prophet had recently received through direct revelation once he saw the current layout of the city. Streets were renamed in a similar manner to how cities in Utah had been organized, with the temple lot at the center of the grid system. It wasn't long before South Temple Street in New Jerusalem was as congested from construction as the one in Salt Lake used to be.

Each of the original Rexburg and Manti groups were given a

portion of the Kansas City area to rehabilitate, including tearing down any unsavory or run-down buildings. Since most of the city was already arranged in city blocks, it was easy to divide the city into wards and stakes. There were several electricians and hydro engineers among the Saints, and it only took them a few days to get the electrical and sewer systems functioning again.

Even details such as garbage collection were assigned and moving forward. In many ways the Saints were quickly living by fairly modern standards, although the popular media that had saturated their daily lives the previous years was noticeably—and gratefully—absent.

Most of the buildings surrounding the temple lot had been damaged by storms and tornadoes, and the Elders of Israel were specifically given the assignment to quickly tear down those buildings so that the construction on the temple could begin as soon as possible. Tad and David were assigned there, and they worked hard six days a week as part of a crew that was dismantling an entire street of buildings, saving the bricks and lumber to use later in the construction of the temple plaza.

Tad persuaded their construction supervisor to allow Jonas and Mitko to be part of their crew, and the four of them made a great team. David and Mitko really enjoyed swinging the sledgehammer, trying to outdo each other in knocking down large sections of wall and ceilings.

Tad and Jonas enjoyed watching them go at it. "I'm too old for that kind of stuff," Tad said, "but they never seem to get tired."

"I'm with you," Jonas said. "I'll just stick to picking up bricks and stacking 2x4s."

The only disappointment for Mitko was that the Coalition soldiers who had been spared in the final battle had chosen not to learn about the gospel and had stayed together in Denver. He couldn't have expected much more from them, and he realized they likely weren't ready to live in a Zion society.

⁂

Tad and David were working hard, and the rest of their family members were, too. Emma, Charles, and Leah were assigned to help get large gardens planted. One of the brethren had found a huge abandoned greenhouse that was filled with a wide variety of seeds and vegetables. Charles in particular really had a knack for gardening, and would spend the entire day cultivating and planting.

Emma had found a functioning desktop computer, and in the evenings she spent time writing about her extended family's experiences in establishing Zion. She wanted to make sure these events were recorded, with the hope that someday they would be of interest to future generations.

With her background as a teacher, Becky was immediately recruited to help organize a gospel-based school curriculum for the younger children. She and others of the so-called "144,000 widows" stayed so busy in creating Zion's educational system that they barely missed their husbands—although they would never admit it.

There were several women who helped watch the youngest children, including little Daniel, and everyone cooperated to make the most of their talents. They had located several elementary schools that were undamaged, and soon their program was off and running.

The biggest adjustment initially was the fact that no one had money—and didn't need any. The bishops oversaw both the temporal and spiritual aspects of each ward, and the Relief Society and priesthood quorums performed their duties.

For the first time in Church history, home teaching and visiting teaching hit 100 percent. As Tad joked, "The biggest miracle here is that the elders are actually visiting their assigned families!"

The Saints were able to prosper in ways they had never imagined, and life was good. The land of Zion was indeed a holy place for the Saints, as it would be for the millions who would yet call it their home.

Chapter 30

As the first arrivals to Independence began their third week of reshaping the city, Josh Brown led his group across the Missouri state line. Mathoni had volunteered to speed ahead and let the Church leaders know they were on their way, so Josh hoped there would be at least a small welcoming committee.

"Only a few more miles," he told the group, and they increased their pace.

Later that afternoon, they turned south toward the temple lot, and Josh could hardly believe his eyes. There were crowds of people lining both sides of the street, and they were cheering loudly.

Suddenly Mathoni popped up next to him. "Everyone is excited to welcome our group," he said. "Our journey from Guatemala is apparently already legendary, and the apostles have requested that everyone stop working the rest of the day so our group can be welcomed properly."

Josh felt a rush of emotion as nearly a year of tremendous effort was coming to a close. The outpouring of love was unexpected and almost overwhelming. The Guatemalan and Hopi Saints could hardly believe this grand reception was for them.

As the Browns reached the temple lot, a young man with dark hair rushed toward them. "President and Sister Brown! Is that really you?"

The Browns turned to see Mitko Petrov standing before them. "Elder Petrov! How did you get here? I thought you had returned to Bulgaria."

Mitko smiled. "It's a long story, but I'm so glad you made it!

I'm actually good friends with Tad and David North, and they've told me what you have been up to. I'm so proud of you."

The celebration lasted through the evening, and then the Browns' group was shown their part of the city. It had once been a middle-class section of Kansas City, but the homes looked like palaces to the Guatemalan and Hopi Saints. They wept for joy and kept asking, "Are these homes really for us?"

The Guatemalan and Hopi men got right to work improving their section of the city, and there was a gladness among the people. Everyone had been under such stress for so long that the absence of it made life even better.

Kim and Josh were given a home right in the midst of "their" people, and they could hardly believe the joy they felt. Kim was now several months along with her pregnancy, but she felt energized, After talking with Becky, she took charge of organizing the same gospel-based school curriculum among the children who had traveled with her, and the women dived right in to help out.

Josh had many ecclesiastical duties to perform as a member of the First Quorum of the Seventy, but it seemed like less work after watching over thousands of people the past several months. He spent a lot of time working with stake presidents and organizing wards into functional units. It was very rewarding as he saw people catch the true spirit of the gospel.

One day he opened his door to find his good friend Elder Smith of the Quorum of the Twelve standing there. "I've been asked to escort you to meet with the First Presidency," Elder Smith said. "Have you been a bad boy?"

Josh shook his head. "Not that I know of."

Elder Smith smiled. "I didn't think so."

Soon Josh was seated alone with the First Presidency, and his palms really started to sweat. As he shook hands with them, the prophet laughed and motioned to his now-moist hand. "There's nothing to worry about, Elder Brown. We've never really had the chance to get to know each other very well, but I've heard splendid things about you, even from clear back when you were a stake president."

"Thank you. I really appreciate that."

The prophet then dismissed his counselors, and Josh got even more nervous. As they closed the door, the prophet looked him in the eyes and said, "As you know, one of our brothers in the Quorum of the Twelve passed away in Rexburg not long ago. We now have a vacancy in the quorum, and the Lord has indicated that you are the one that should fill that spot."

Josh was momentarily speechless. "I'm so honored. It doesn't seem very long ago that I was in Spanish Fork serving as my ward's high priest group secretary. I was content to stay in that calling for a long time."

The prophet laughed. "See? That's your problem—you humbly serve wherever you are asked and never seek for a position. Among other reasons, I'm sure that is why the Lord has chosen you." The prophet got a twinkle in his eye. "But I understand your feelings. There are times I wish I could go back to being on the Activities Committee with my wife, like when we were newlyweds. But the Lord had other plans."

The prophet called his counselors back into the room and ordained Josh an apostle, pronouncing marvelous blessings upon his head that he could scarcely comprehend. He emerged from the meeting in a daze, but rushed home to tell Kim the news. The First Presidency issued an announcement about his call over the Church satellite system, and soon every group of Saints throughout the world knew that Elder Joshua Brown was the newest member of the Quorum of the Twelve Apostles.

Josh quickly received several new assignments and spent long hours immersed in the work of the Lord. He was particularly intrigued by his assignment to oversee the development of new technologies that would help New Jerusalem take huge steps forward in terms of energy conservation and efficiency. The Lord had brought several leading scientists to Zion among these first groups of Saints, and as they had waited in the frozen mountains the past few months, their minds had been opened to many new possibilities, and now they were eager to share the inspiration they had received.

What amazed Josh is how one scientist who had been a professor at BYU had an idea that tied in perfectly with a concept that one of his Guatemalan Saints had developed. As these scientists met each day and worked together on their ideas, it was becoming clear that New Jerusalem was going to be a city well prepared to enter the millennial era. Josh's mind could hardly comprehend what these men and women were discussing, but their preliminary outlines concerning solar energy alone would revolutionize the entire city—and the world.

Josh finally got a break one evening and went to a vacant building that was being torn down. He made his way to the third floor and scanned the entire area. There were families walking together or working together in their yards, and the trees were sprouting their leaves in orderly rows along the streets. One overwhelming feeling prevailed—peace.

Josh realized the Lord had fulfilled all of his promises. The city was only in the beginning stages, but he knew he was looking out at a celestial city that would stand through the millennial reign of their Savior and beyond.

He thought back on the strange twists his life had taken over the past two years, and he realized what a unique friendship he had with Mathoni, a fellow disciple of the Lord. He hadn't seen Mathoni for several weeks, but he knew he was somewhere in the world preparing other people to create Zion-based cities. But he knew he would see him again—they still had a busload of plates to deliver to the prophet.

Despite all of these wonderful blessings, Josh admitted to himself there was still something gnawing at him. He knew the apostles had numerous ecclesiastical duties, but the main duty of an apostle was to serve as a special witness of Jesus Christ. Josh had an unshakable testimony of the gospel and the plan of salvation, but was that enough?

Every day since his ordination to the apostleship he had prayed fervently for a definite confirmation from the Lord that he truly was meant to fulfill that calling. Although he had felt the Holy Ghost confirm it in his heart several times, it just didn't feel sufficient for the magnitude of the position.

Josh stepped away from the edge of the building and kneeled in a dark corner. He prayed as he never had before, thanking the Lord for all he had been given, and asking once again for a confirmation of his calling as an apostle.

"Joshua."

He opened his eyes to see a brilliant light hovering near him and looked up to see the handsome face of someone he had known throughout the eternities—the Lord Jesus Christ.

The Savior extended his hand, and Josh reached out for it.

"Testify of me," the Savior said. "You are a chosen servant, and I will always be with you."

Josh bowed his head. "I will do whatever is asked of me. All I have ever sought is to do thy will."

"I know, and I am well-pleased with you. I am also pleased with the diligence of the Saints in building this city. They are becoming united in purpose, and the day will soon come when I shall walk among them, as will other faithful servants of this dispensation who labored so diligently."

The Savior then placed his hand on Josh's head and pronounced a blessing that no mortal man could repeat, speaking of future assignments that awaited him. The magnitude of the blessing left Josh both fascinated and humbled to the core.

Then the Savior was gone, and Josh fell back, feeling nearly consumed by the Spirit. With a glimpse of what awaited him, he now felt fortified to face it.

⁂

That same day, Doug climbed atop a hill in Paterson, New Jersey, where he had served his mission many years earlier. The day was clear, and he could see Manhattan in the distance. The skyline had certainly changed over the past couple of years, with large gaps where magnificent buildings once stood. But even now, a few skyscrapers were somehow still upright, gleaming in the sun.

Soon after leaving Denver, Doug had felt compelled to come straight to this area. Many families he had baptized long ago were still living near Manhattan when the government fell apart, and the Spirit testified to him that some of them were still here—and still loved by the Lord.

Doug kneeled for several minutes, asking for guidance and protection. He knew that the urban streets he had once walked were probably meaner than ever, filled with uncivilized groups who would strike first and ask questions later. But the time had come to fulfill his calling, and he felt strangely calm.

He followed the trail down the hill and headed east toward the skyscrapers, trusting that he would be led to the pure in heart.

Into the Future

Although New Jerusalem has been established, there is much work left to be completed by the Saints before the Second Coming of the Savior.

The celestial city will continue to expand in marvelous ways, and the temple will soon be completed, followed by a dedication of heavenly proportions.

Other developments include:

How Doug's mission as one of the 144,000 high priests brings unexpected blessings to his extended family.

The effort led by Jonas to reclaim Salt Lake City for the Saints.

The remarkable journey of the Lost Ten Tribes as they return from the north countries to receive their temple blessings in New Jerusalem.

Read about these events and many others as the *Standing in Holy Places* series continues in *Book Three: The Rise of Zion.*

About the Author

Chad Daybell has written more than 20 books for the LDS market. He is known for his bestselling novels such as *Chasing Paradise* and *The Emma Trilogy*, as well as his non-fiction books for youth, including *The Aaronic Priesthood* and *The Youth of Zion*. He and his wife Tammy also created the *Tiny Talks* series for Primary children.

Chad has worked in the publishing business for the past two decades. He is currently the president of Spring Creek Book Company, one of the leading LDS publishing firms.

Visit **www.springcreekbooks.com** to see the company's lineup of popular titles.

Learn about Chad and the upcoming volumes in the *Standing in Holy Places* series at his personal website **www.cdaybell.com**.